Have a
time!

A GOOD DEMON
is hard to find

Kate Moseman

A Good Demon Is Hard to Find

Copyright © 2020 by Kate Moseman

All rights reserved. No part of this book may be reproduced or used in any manner without written permission of the copyright owner except for the use of quotations in a book review.

This is a work of fiction. Names, characters, places, and incidents either are the product of the author's imagination or are used fictitiously. Any resemblance to actual persons, living or dead, events, or locales is entirely coincidental.

First Edition

ISBN 978-1-7345144-0-7 (ebook)
ISBN 978-1-7345144-1-4 (paperback)

Published by:
Fortunella Press

*Subscribe to Kate Moseman's newsletter at
katemoseman.com for exclusive freebies,
and be the first to know about upcoming releases!*

*Subscribe to Kate Moseman's newsletter at
katemoseman.com for exclusive freebies,
and be the first to know about upcoming releases!*

Dedicated to all the apostates

PART I

ERIN

PART I
ERIN

1

Erin hurled another armful of clothes out the front door. "Take your stupid shirts"—she paused to reload, scooping up another pile beside the doorway—"and your stupid pants, and get lost." The pants followed the shirts out the door, collapsing on the lawn like a flock of fainting birds under the rapidly dimming sky.

It was lucky he'd left a few things behind after the divorce—they made great ammunition.

"Be reasonable, Erin," said Mark, her ex-husband. "Can't we discuss this like adults? I only came over because you continue to refuse to answer your phone, and having this conversation at church is not exactly a good idea."

Erin turned back into the house, found a shoe, and hurled it over her shoulder without looking. It narrowly missed Mark and instead nailed the driver's side door of his cherry red convertible. She found the matching shoe, turned around, aimed, and flung it end over end to join its mate.

"Watch it!"

"Oh, did I ding your midlife crisis-mobile? I'm sorry," said Erin, without a shred of sincerity. She tucked her hair behind her ears and crossed her arms.

"I wish you wouldn't make a scene," said Mark.

"Really? I'd prefer you weren't a cheating dog, but you get what you get, right?"

Mark rolled his eyes and leaned back against the car in the driveway. "Look, Erin, all I'm asking you to do is find someplace else to worship, okay? I know you're only going to church to keep your mom off your back."

He might have been right, but that didn't mean he deserved reasonability in return. Erin glanced around, looking for more things to throw. She spied a stack of Mark's exercise DVDs. She picked them up and flung them one at a time, like frisbees, into the yard. "I. Said. Get. Lost."

An ancient Pomeranian shuffled to the doorway and peered out into the soft light of the setting sun.

Erin picked up the dog.

"How's Nancy Drew?" said Mark, in a transparent attempt to defuse the situation.

"She's great. She never liked you, anyway," said Erin, scratching her behind the ears.

Mark looked upwards as if asking for strength. "Erin, I'm asking you. Can you please stop going to our church? Wouldn't that make things easier for you?"

"Are you kidding?" said Erin, carefully setting Nancy Drew down on the tile floor of the entryway. "You don't want to make things easier for me. You want to make it easier for you and Genevieve."

"Genevieve has just as much right to be there as you do," said Mark.

"Does she? Kind of uncomfortable to be reminded of your sin every single Sunday, isn't it."

"Now you're just being difficult." Mark threw his hands up.

"Maybe I like going to church with my ex-husband and the woman he cheated on me with. If it bothers you so much, why don't you find a different church?" She stepped onto the covered porch and carefully shut the door behind her, to keep Nancy Drew from making an escape.

"Come on, Erin."

"It's 'Come on, Erin,' this and 'Be reasonable, Erin,' that when you want something, isn't it?" Erin took a barefooted step forward.

Mark took a step back.

"You don't have any claim on me. Not that you ever had any real say over what I do in the first place—but whatever I owed your sorry ass evaporated when you cheated on me and made a mockery of our wedding vows. I'll go to church, or not, if I want to, for any reason or no reason at all. So you can take your stupid shirts and your ugly khaki pants and drive your ridiculous compensation car all the way to hell." Erin pointed her finger at Mark. "May the Lord forsake you and the Devil take you!"

As she spoke, the last sliver of the sun disappeared behind the western horizon.

She whirled and went inside the house, slamming the door behind her and stomping away before remembering to turn back and lock it.

The bolt slammed home loudly, echoing in the sparsely furnished house.

Erin leaned against the door and slid down to the floor.

Nancy Drew shuffled over and stared at her with rheumy eyes.

"Oh, Nancy," said Erin, running her fingers down the dog's back. A terrible pressure welled up in her chest as she tried to hold back the tears. They escaped anyway, like water from a glass filled to the brim, dripping down her cheeks.

Mark had seemed like a good idea at the time. His self-assuredness, relentlessly on display at the local steakhouse where they went for most of their dates, provided a sense of solidity in a world that felt like it was shifting under her feet. After six months of dating, he'd asked for her hand over the steaks he'd ordered well-done, and she'd answered "Yes" without hesitation.

After the wedding, when they settled into a well-done routine of perfectly correct married life, she put aside the feelings that didn't quite fit into her new life with Mark.

It shouldn't matter that steaks were starting to make her queasy—or that church services inevitably brought on a sense of anxiety. She had chosen him, and he had chosen her.

It should have been enough.

Erin wiped away the tears with the back of her hand and stood up. She peeked out of the dusty window blinds and was relieved to find that Mark had gathered his things and left. She headed for the kitchen, Nancy Drew trailing her hopefully.

"Here, girl," said Erin, offering Nancy a dog biscuit from the glass container on the Formica countertop.

Nancy, blind as a bat, nosed around until her snout bumped the biscuit, at which point she snapped it up with doggy enthusiasm.

"How is it? Good?" Erin retrieved a second biscuit from the jar and eyed it. She tentatively nibbled a corner. "Not bad," she mused. "I can't get any lower than this, Nancy. My husband left me for another woman and I'm eating dog biscuits while talking to a mostly deaf dog."

Nancy tried to focus in Erin's general direction.

Erin handed Nancy the nibbled biscuit. "Only slightly used. But you won't mind, will you, girl?" She kneeled and patted the dog. "Is it too early for bed?"

Nancy sat down heavily on her hindquarters, as if she was too tired to keep holding them up.

"I feel the same way," said Erin. She rose and crossed to the pantry, where she considered a dusty bottle of red wine half-hidden behind a stash of paper towel rolls. They never drank wine, so the bottle—a gift from a wedding guest—had sat untouched for years. Erin retrieved it and rummaged in a drawer for something to open it with. A multi-purpose kitchen tool revealed a fold-out corkscrew that served the purpose.

Lacking a wine glass, Erin poured the wine into an insulated plastic tumbler and retreated into her bedroom with the tumbler and the bottle.

She drank a big swallow of wine and coughed. Perhaps this wasn't the best idea.

Then again, she didn't have any better ideas. She took another sip, set the tumbler and bottle on the nightstand, changed into her pajamas, and crawled under the covers.

Two tumblers of wine later, her head buzzed like a beehive. She should have eaten something to soak up the wine, something more than a nibble of dog biscuit, but it was too late.

Erin rolled onto her side and closed her eyes. The room spun. She searched her mind for comforting thoughts to chase away the impending nightmares and found nothing.

Instead, she recalled her last words to Mark. *The Lord forsake you and the Devil take you.*

Erin shuddered with embarrassment. Could she be any more childish? She cringed into her pillow and pulled the covers tighter, willing herself to go to sleep.

With her eyes still closed, and her mind drifting in a state between wakefulness and unconsciousness, a frisson crawled over her skin from the top of her head all the way to her toes, wiping away the tension in her body as it rippled through her. If this was a dream, she didn't want to wake up. It was far more pleasant than her current reality.

A sound like an unfurled bolt of silk brought her to the edge of awareness. She dreamily observed a pair of gray feathered wings unfolding over her. Instead of feeling frightened, she felt sheltered—safe—as she tumbled the rest of the way into the darkness of sleep.

2

The phone on the nightstand rang.

Erin groaned and rolled across the bed. She grabbed the phone and mashed the button to pick up. "Hello?"

"Well, hello there. You sound rough."

It was Joyce, Erin's mother.

"Mom?" Erin blinked at the clock. 8:00 a.m. on the dot.

"What are you doing in bed, honey? Weren't you and Mark always up with the chickens?"

"Mark isn't around anymore, Mom, and there never were any chickens. Unless he was hiding those from me, too."

"It's amazing how you can still make jokes about it," said Joyce.

"Would you rather I made death threats? It would be more satisfying," said Erin, lying back on a pillow and closing her eyes.

"Don't say that. It sounds so un-Christian. Besides, you and Mark were a great couple. I just don't understand what went so wrong."

Erin sat straight up and triggered a massive pain in her head. "A great couple? Are you kidding? He cheated on me, Mom. We're divorced. There is no 'you and Mark' anymore." She rubbed her eyes. "And if we're going to talk about being 'un-Christian,' how about we talk about Mark's behavior instead of my reaction to it?" Erin smacked her lips together, trying to work some saliva into the foul-tasting desert of her mouth.

"Of course, darling," she trilled. "Have you eaten? What are you making for breakfast?"

"No, Mom, I haven't eaten. I just woke up. And I don't know what I'm making for breakfast."

"Did you ever make Mark breakfast?"

"Oh, my God, Mom! Lay off."

Her mom clicked her tongue. "You know, honey, men like to feel taken care of."

"Like little boys," Erin said, standing up and stretching.

"Exactly! You do understand, but for some reason you never follow through on my advice."

"Can't imagine why," said Erin, sliding her feet into her slippers. "Mom, I gotta go get ready for church."

"You're not afraid to see Mark?"

"Mark is dead to me."

"That's a little extreme, don't you think?"

"No."

"Well, wear your good dress. And put on some makeup."

"Sure, Mom. Bye now." Erin hung up the phone and hurled it onto the unmade bed. She didn't even know why she bothered going to church anymore. Habit, maybe. Or just a desire to make Mark and Genevieve squirm.

A crash from the direction of the kitchen made Erin jump.

Nancy Drew looked up from the floor next to the foot of the bed.

Erin picked up the half-full bottle of wine, ready to throw it. Nancy stood up and swished her tail back and forth.

They crept into the hallway leading to the kitchen.

"Who's there?" called Erin. "Is that you, Mark?"

"I'm sorry," called a male voice. "I was just looking for a mug and I knocked a plate off the shelf. How do you like your coffee?"

Definitely not Mark.

Erin stepped into the kitchen and confronted a nattily dressed, youngish man in a dark red suit and bow tie. "Who are you?" She deftly flipped the wine bottle up to hold it like a club, but forgot that it was still half full of wine and poured it all over herself.

The man rubbed his closely-trimmed salt and pepper beard. "Are you in the habit of pouring wine all over yourself, or is this a special occasion?"

"Get out of my house, or I'll call the police!" She brandished the now-empty bottle as her fuzzy slippers slowly absorbed the puddle of wine.

"Why don't we start with introductions? Hi, I'm Andromalius, but you can call me 'Andy' for short." He smiled, exposing a row of gleaming white teeth, and held out his hand to shake.

He didn't seem like a murderer—but then, would he? Erin backed away. "I don't care what your name is. You need to leave right now."

He put his hand down. "But you invited me."

"I invited you?"

"You invited me," he said, as if he had received an engraved invitation by mail, signature required upon delivery. He seemed hurt.

"How did I invite you?"

"Oh, you remember," he said, waving his hand airily.

"No. I don't!"

He sighed and took a small step closer to her.

Nancy Drew, noticing that he had also moved closer to the jar of dog biscuits, approached him expectantly.

"'The Lord forsake you and the Devil take you,' remember? Does that ring any bells?"

Erin lowered the wine bottle. "What did you say?"

"I said"—he stood up straight and pointed his finger at her in a way that unmistakably reminded her of herself—"The Lord forsake you and the Devil take you!"

"How did you—is this some kind of joke? Did Mark put you up to this?"

The man looked offended. "He most certainly did not."

"Who are you?"

"I told you."

"Andro-something," said Erin.

"Andromalius, a mighty Great Earl of Hell. But you can call me Andy." He inclined his head.

"A great earl of what?"

"Hell. Great Earl of Hell. But I don't believe in standing on ceremony. You don't need to curtsy, or make a sacrifice, or anything."

Was he trying to look modest? "You're not from hell. You're just some maniac who broke into my house."

"Is that so? Watch this." He snapped his fingers and wings—impossibly large, gray wings flecked with white—exploded from behind his shoulders, filling the width of the kitchen and making a sound like an oversized umbrella snapping open.

Erin staggered backward. "Oh, my God!"

"Wrong direction," said Andromalius, Great Earl of Hell, and pointed downward.

Nancy Drew barked and tottered in a circle.

"Put them away, you're scaring the dog," said Erin, her voice shaking.

"Oh! Sorry, dog." He snapped his fingers and the wings retracted, then disappeared. He retrieved a dog biscuit from the jar and held it out to the dog.

Nancy Drew took it and lay down, crunching the biscuit happily.

"He's probably hungry," said Andromalius, Great Earl of Hell.

"She," said Erin, absently. "Nancy Drew."

He stared at her for a very long moment. "So, she's Nancy Drew, you're Erin, and I'm—"

"From hell."

"Just call me Andy."

"Andy. And you're the devil," she said.

"Not the devil. A demon. Can I get you a chair? You look a bit peaky."

Erin glanced down at herself. Her pajamas and slippers were soaked in red wine. She was probably puffy-faced, too, from the wine of the night before. She pressed one hand to her throbbing head.

"Fear not, a demon is here to help you out!" He gently removed the wine bottle from her hand and steered her into a chair next to the kitchen table. Then he made jazz hands, as if to say "Ta-da!"

"But demons don't really exist. And if they do, they're evil. They make people do bad things."

"Wrong! Humans don't need any help doing bad things. How about that coffee?" said Andy.

"I don't want your demon coffee."

Andy examined the coffee bag. "It's not my fault you buy pre-ground. And anyway, you summoned me."

"I did not," Erin said.

"You did so. When you cursed your lover." He waggled his eyebrows at her.

Erin picked up the wine bottle from the table and pointed it at him. "Ugh. Don't call him that."

"Your beau? Your *inamorato*?"

"Are you insane?"

"I don't socialize much," admitted Andy.

"So, I called up a demon to curse my ex-husband and now he's here in my kitchen and won't leave." She set the wine bottle down with a bang.

"In a nutshell. What were you thinking about in terms of the devil taking him? I'm assuming something really big and splashy. Hang on, let me get my notebook." He reached into his inside coat pocket and pulled out an expensive-looking notepad and an old-fashioned pen. He flipped open the notebook. "Okay, go."

"I don't want demon help, Mr. Demon."

"It's Andy. Or Andromalius if you're feeling formal. And of course you want help, you laid the curse in the first place. What type of revenge shall we start with? Boils? An unscratchable itch? That's always a good one." He looked at her hopefully.

"I'll pray you away."

"Go ahead and try," he said cheerfully.

Erin eyed him skeptically. She folded her hands and closed her eyes. "Dear Lord, please remove this demon from my kitchen. Amen." She opened her eyes and gazed upon the very much still-present demon.

Andy cleared his throat. "Sorry about that."

"Why didn't it work?"

He poured water into the coffee machine. "There's a part of you that wants me to fulfill my duty."

"Your duty? Demon duty?" Erin laughed with a hysterical edge.

He pointed the coffee scoop at her. "You're the one who called for demonic help."

"I didn't know the universe would take me seriously. So, what, you help me get revenge on Mark somehow, and then you'll leave?"

The coffee burbled into the pot. Andy didn't respond until he had filled a mug and placed it in front of Erin. "Exactly."

Erin picked up the mug and looked inside it as if she expected it to contain spiders. "Cream, two sugars," she said.

He wordlessly collected the mug, added a shot of half-and-half, stirred in two teaspoons of sugar, and returned it to her. He slid into the seat across from her at the kitchen table. "Do we have a deal?"

She sipped her coffee and looked into his eyes, which were a deep brown color with almost imperceptible flecks of garnet. "Do I have a choice?"

"You always have a choice," he said.

She set down her mug. "What? I told you to get out when I first laid eyes on you."

"You told me that before you had a chance to think about it." His voice slid into a lower register, which did strange things to her ability to think clearly. "Ask me to go and I will. I'll never darken your doorstep again. But I think"—he ran one fingertip around the rim of his own mug of coffee—"I think we might have some fun with this."

Erin stared at the demon seated at her kitchen table. Her gaze swept over his ridiculously combed hair, his well-trimmed beard, and his absurd red bow tie. "I got rid of my husband," she said. "And I suppose I could get rid of you, too. If I needed to."

"You certainly could," he murmured.

"But you can't do anything without my approval," she added.

"Wouldn't dream of it," he said, flashing his perfect teeth.

"And you'd have to stay out of my hair."

"But of course," he said. "Do we have a deal?" He reached his hand across the table.

She took his hand. It was warmer than she expected, almost but not quite hot to the touch. "It's a deal."

3

"Is that what you're wearing?" Andy asked.

Erin, fresh out of a shower and facing the mirror examining herself in a navy tea-length dress, looked over her shoulder at him. "What do you mean by that?"

"You should make him regret he left you. Show a little leg or something."

"You may not be familiar with the concept, demon, but I'm going to church. You know, a house of God?"

"Why would God have a problem with your leg?"

"As far as I know, God doesn't have a problem with my leg."

"Then why not show it off?" Andy extended one trouser-clad leg in a way that was clearly intended to be enticing.

"Why does a demon sound like my mother?" Erin muttered.

"Does your mother want you to show some leg?"

"No! I mean, sort of. At first, she wanted me to give up on the divorce and get back together with Mark."

Andy approached her from behind as she faced the mirror. He peered at her in the reflection. "Do you want to get back together with him?" His expressive eyes widened.

"Of course not. He's a dog." Erin smoothed the front of the dress. "Sorry, Nancy. No offense," she added in an aside to the dog, who had returned to her spot at the foot of the bed.

"Well, then." Andy patted her shoulders in a comradely way. "What shall we do first? We discussed boils and itching, but an audience opens up all sorts of exciting possibilities." He whipped out his notebook and flipped through the pages.

Erin laughed. "You think you're going to church with me? You can't even set foot in there."

Andy smirked. "I am a Great Earl of Hell and the Discoverer of Wickedness. You'd be surprised where I can go."

"Oh, what, anywhere with wickedness?" Erin raised her eyebrows.

Andy bowed. *"Naturellement."* He turned to Erin's closet and rummaged enthusiastically, flinging clothing across the bed.

"Wouldn't people see you?"

"Only if I wanted them to." He waggled a little black dress in her direction. "Can I interest you in this chic number?"

Erin shook her head. "There's nothing you can do there, anyway."

"Fine." Andy pouted. "Can we at least do your hair?"

Erin looked at him like he'd sprouted an extra head instead of a set of wings. "A demonic hairstyle?"

"Don't knock it till you try it. Sit down."

Erin lowered herself into the chair facing the vanity mirror.

Andy reached into another pocket and retrieved a handful of silver hairpins. "Hold still."

Erin felt his warm fingers slide up from the top of her neck deep into the hair on the back of her head. He gripped and twisted in one smooth movement, gathering stray locks with his free hand and pinning them artfully into the twist.

It all happened so quickly that Erin barely had time to register the goose bumps that rose on her arms. She couldn't, however, avoid the sight of her reddened cheeks in the mirror, especially when his warm hands brushed past them to arrange a loose tendril or two.

"There," said Andy. "That's better."

"Thanks," said Erin, and tore her gaze away from the mirror to stare at the surface of the vanity instead. "What will you do while I'm gone?"

"Talk to Nancy. Stretch my wings. Come up with plans to torture your ex-husband."

Erin smiled ruefully. "Maybe I should have fixed him breakfast more often."

"How often did he fix you breakfast?" said Andy.

Erin searched her memory and came up with nothing.

In her silence, Andy got his answer. "You're well rid of him. More coffee before you go?"

Erin parked in the lot adjacent to the church and took several calming breaths before opening the car door. She picked up her Bible—with a slim romance novel tucked inside—and joined the trickle of parishioners making their way into the building.

If she was lucky, she could avoid her mother until the last possible second.

She threaded her way through the lobby, past the ushers, into the sanctuary, and down the aisle flanked by sturdy wooden pews. She took a seat in the back, next to the aisle, far from the front rows preferred by her mother—and, of course, Mark.

"Darling! What are you doing here? Come sit up front," said her mother, who swept up from behind and seized her arm.

Since diving under the pews wasn't an option, Erin freed herself and spoke in a quiet but firm tone. "Not now, mother. Don't make a scene."

"Nonsense. Who's making a scene? Can't I sit with my only daughter?"

"Sit here, then."

"And miss Pastor Patrick? You know I can't see that far."

"You can watch him on the video projection screen, Mom."

"Fine," her mother huffed and plopped down next to Erin. "You win. Oh look, there's Mark and Genevieve!"

"Quiet!" Erin gritted out. She pretended not to watch them make their way down to the front.

"She looks a little chubby," her mother observed.

"Mother, can you not?"

"I'm just saying."

The service began with music, followed by prayer. Erin wondered if God would forgive her for speaking in anger.

And for accidentally conjuring a demon.

And for letting said demon do her hair.

Perhaps, she decided, she should save up all her sins and ask forgiveness for all of them at once, when this was all over.

She paid less attention than she should during the sermon, which was on the subject of "Fresh Starts," because she was too busy trying to watch Mark and Genevieve without it looking like

Erin felt his warm fingers slide up from the top of her neck deep into the hair on the back of her head. He gripped and twisted in one smooth movement, gathering stray locks with his free hand and pinning them artfully into the twist.

It all happened so quickly that Erin barely had time to register the goose bumps that rose on her arms. She couldn't, however, avoid the sight of her reddened cheeks in the mirror, especially when his warm hands brushed past them to arrange a loose tendril or two.

"There," said Andy. "That's better."

"Thanks," said Erin, and tore her gaze away from the mirror to stare at the surface of the vanity instead. "What will you do while I'm gone?"

"Talk to Nancy. Stretch my wings. Come up with plans to torture your ex-husband."

Erin smiled ruefully. "Maybe I should have fixed him breakfast more often."

"How often did he fix you breakfast?" said Andy.

Erin searched her memory and came up with nothing.

In her silence, Andy got his answer. "You're well rid of him. More coffee before you go?"

Erin parked in the lot adjacent to the church and took several calming breaths before opening the car door. She picked up her Bible—with a slim romance novel tucked inside—and joined the trickle of parishioners making their way into the building.

If she was lucky, she could avoid her mother until the last possible second.

She threaded her way through the lobby, past the ushers, into the sanctuary, and down the aisle flanked by sturdy wooden pews. She took a seat in the back, next to the aisle, far from the front rows preferred by her mother—and, of course, Mark.

"Darling! What are you doing here? Come sit up front," said her mother, who swept up from behind and seized her arm.

Since diving under the pews wasn't an option, Erin freed herself and spoke in a quiet but firm tone. "Not now, mother. Don't make a scene."

"Nonsense. Who's making a scene? Can't I sit with my only daughter?"

"Sit here, then."

"And miss Pastor Patrick? You know I can't see that far."

"You can watch him on the video projection screen, Mom."

"Fine," her mother huffed and plopped down next to Erin. "You win. Oh look, there's Mark and Genevieve!"

"Quiet!" Erin gritted out. She pretended not to watch them make their way down to the front.

"She looks a little chubby," her mother observed.

"Mother, can you not?"

"I'm just saying."

The service began with music, followed by prayer. Erin wondered if God would forgive her for speaking in anger.

And for accidentally conjuring a demon.

And for letting said demon do her hair.

Perhaps, she decided, she should save up all her sins and ask forgiveness for all of them at once, when this was all over.

She paid less attention than she should during the sermon, which was on the subject of "Fresh Starts," because she was too busy trying to watch Mark and Genevieve without it looking like she was watching them. The video projection screen helped a lot, since the camera frequently panned over the front rows.

When the sermon concluded, the ushers stood to prepare to hand out the offering plates after the next hymn.

She glanced at the ushers on her side of the sanctuary—and froze.

One of them wasn't an usher. It was Andy.

He waved at her.

Her mouth fell open. She looked around to see if anyone had noticed a demon in a red suit and bow tie.

No one else acted as if anything were amiss.

Andy walked to the front of the church. He pointed at Mark, and then gave Erin a double thumbs-up signal.

She shook her head vigorously, not knowing what he was up to but that it was almost certainly a very bad idea.

The audience stood to sing the hymn. The camera panned over the front rows, but Andy was invisible to the camera. Erin looked from the big screen to the scene unfolding in real life as Andy briefly ducked out of her view.

And then Mark's pants fell off.

The congregation gasped.

Erin could see Mark's novelty "Check Your Fly" fishing boxers clearly on the big screen before a red-faced Mark pulled up his trousers. The camera quickly pivoted away.

A smattering of giggles broke out across the room, quickly muffled but unmistakable.

Erin's mother pressed one hand to her chest and used her other hand to fan herself with a folded church program.

Andy walked nonchalantly up the aisle and leaned over the side of Erin's pew to whisper in her ear. "Caught with his pants down, am I right?" He had the nerve to grin at her before sauntering out of the church.

Erin didn't know whether to laugh, cry, or sprint after the retreating demon and strangle him with her bare hands.

Could you strangle a demon?

There was nothing else to do but silently fume her way through the remainder of the service, until it finally wrapped up with a rousing—and unfortunately ironic—version of the old hymn "It Is Well."

The moment the congregation rose from the pews, Erin tore down the aisle in pursuit of Andy, with her mother's cries at her abrupt departure echoing behind her. She crossed the parking lot at a near run and found Andy sitting inside her car with the music turned up so loud she could hear it outside the vehicle.

She tugged at the driver's side door handle, realized the door was locked, and yanked her purse off her shoulder to rummage in the bottom for the keys. Only then did she realize that the car was already running.

Andy leaned across and popped the lock from the inside.

She slid into the driver's seat, slammed the door, and mashed the button to turn off the car stereo. "Just what did you think you were doing? And how did you get my keys?"

"You left them in the car. In addition to being a Great Earl of Hell with authority over wickedness and revenge, I am also the Finder of Lost Things. You're welcome," he said.

"'You're welcome'? Are you kidding me?"

Andy turned to face her with an impish expression. "You realize you look like you're shouting at no one?"

Erin growled and threw the car into reverse. "Why don't you just fly home, demon?"

"Because this is much more fun," he said.

"Not for me," Erin spat.

"You didn't like it?" His eyes widened innocently.

"That's not the point!"

"You did like it," he said, clasping his hands together with deep satisfaction. "I knew you would."

"I thought you were staying home to stretch your wings."

"I was. I did! But then I came up with this great idea, so—"

"So you barged in without asking me."

His cheery demeanor faltered. "I thought you'd be happy."

She slammed the steering wheel with one hand as she peeled out of the parking lot. "You don't think you were overstepping just a bit? Do you even know what happened to me before you showed up?"

"No," said Andy in a small voice.

Erin laughed. "You're a supernatural being. How do you not know?"

He sank down further in the passenger's seat. "That's not how it works."

"Oh, yeah, Mr. Demon? Then maybe you should explain how it works. Better yet, maybe you should be quiet and listen for a bit."

"Okay," said a very contrite Great Earl of Hell.

4

Erin pulled into the deserted parking lot of a fast food chain that was closed on Sundays.

"I can't talk about this and drive at the same time," said Erin.

"You want me to drive?" said Andy.

"Do you know how to drive?"

"No."

They sat in silence.

Andy peered up at the billboard overhead.

Erin propped her arm against the door and leaned her head on her hand. She closed her eyes. "Go ahead, then. Explain to me how this whole demon thing works."

"I was just going to sit quietly and listen," said Andy.

"No, go ahead. I want to hear this first."

Andy inhaled a deep breath and blew it out slowly. "What do you want to know?"

"Surprise me."

"I'm sorry I upset you."

Erin waved the apology away. "It's fine. You meant well. Which is kind of surprising, considering you're a demon and all."

"I was just trying to do my job."

"Your job." Erin looked at him skeptically.

"I don't get work often," he said.

"What are you, some sort of freelance demon? How are you not busy all the time?"

"Demons have always been obsolete, Erin. Humans don't need demons for inspiration. They never did. You manage to do horrible things all on your own. I've spent ages just—I don't know—mucking about. Waiting for the call."

"And I called."

"And you called. So here I am. Trying to do a bad day's work in a world that doesn't need me anymore."

"If you don't have anything to do anymore, couldn't you"—Erin paused, searching for the most delicate way to phrase it—"go back?"

Andy snorted. "It doesn't work that way."

"Why not?"

"Well, first of all, from what I've heard about Hell, it doesn't sound like a great place to be. Secondly, I've never been there and wouldn't even know how to get there."

Erin looked at him with undisguised surprise. "You've never been there? But you're a demon."

"I'm almost as tethered to Earth as you are. I don't remember anything else, no matter how far back I go."

Would it be rude to ask his age? Instead, she settled for a less pointed question. "If you're stuck here, what do you do with your time?"

"Wander around. Learn things. I took a massage class last year." He perked up. "Do you know what trigger points are?"

"Yes. No. Not really. Don't change the subject."

"Come on, I'll show you. Unbuckle yourself." He turned in his seat to face her.

"How did you get the money to take a class?"

"I'm the Finder of Lost Things, remember? Money turns up all the time." He reached under the car seat and pulled out a quarter. "See?"

"Convenient." Erin's hand drifted to her seat belt buckle. What was she thinking? You can't accept a massage from a demon you've just met.

Right?

"Look, Andy, I'm sure you meant well. But I don't need your help to get back at Mark." She stole at glance at Andy.

A small smile played around his lips.

She hadn't noticed that his lips were so finely shaped.

"Of course you don't. But wouldn't it be fun to have help?" He leaned toward her ever so slightly.

In the close space of the car, he smelled like cinnamon and smoke.

She unbuckled her seatbelt and turned awkwardly toward the driver's side door. "Maybe," she said, sweeping her hair off her back and pulling it over one shoulder.

He placed his hands lightly on her shoulders. His thumbs kneaded her shoulder blades as his fingertips pressed away the tension in the thick muscles of her shoulders.

Erin felt her shoulders come down from where she had been unconsciously holding them up. His touch really was quite fantastic, and the added heat of his hands melted the tightness away.

She pushed away the strangeness of receiving a shoulder massage from a demon, and leaned back into his touch.

"See? I'm helping you already. A little TLC, and you'll be right as rain and fighting fit, ready to give your ex-husband the humiliation he deserves."

Erin bit her lip to stop a deep sigh from escaping. Slowly, she relaxed until her head tilted sideways onto the driver's seat headrest. Her eyes drifted closed.

Andy continued massaging her shoulders thoroughly with exquisitely intuitive hands.

A knock at the window startled Erin so badly she jumped and banged her knee against the steering wheel.

A uniformed police officer stood next to the car, peering into the window at Erin and making a sign to roll down the window.

In a flash, Erin realized what she must have looked like: sick, drunk, or despondent, lolling sideways against the seat of the car with no one else in sight, considering the demon's currently awkward state of invisibility. She rolled down the window.

"You all right, miss?" asked the officer. He leaned down and looked around the inside of the car, probably in hopes of spotting drug paraphernalia or an open container of alcohol.

"Oh, yes, officer. I was on my way home and I felt a little tired, so I stopped to rest for a minute. I'm fine. Really." Erin opened her eyes wide and hoped that she looked alert, sober, and nonthreatening. She didn't dare look behind her to see what Andy was up to.

Probably making bunny ears behind her head.

"You sure you don't need a doctor or something?" The police officer looked genuinely concerned.

"Oh, no. Really. I'm fine." She was repeating herself out of sheer nervousness.

"Okay, then. Take care, now. You have a good day."

"You too, officer. Thank you." She rolled up the window and faced forward.

Andy snickered.

"Shut up, demon," Erin said as she turned the key in the ignition.

He patted her shoulder. "We're getting into trouble already. Can't you see? This is going to be great!"

Erin's cheeks flamed as she turned back onto the main road.

"I am sorry I didn't get to finish, though," added Andy in a more thoughtful tone. "How about when we get home?"

"When 'we' get home? Who said you were staying at my house?"

"I won't be a bother," said the demon.

Erin gripped the steering wheel even tighter.

Andy relented. "I'm only teasing. I'll stay out of your way. I'll make the coffee. I'll even do the washing up. Whatever you like. All the shoulder massages you can possibly handle. And we'll make the best revenge plan ever, I promise."

At the stoplight before her neighborhood, Erin turned to look at Andy.

He looked back at her with undisguised mischief in his eyes.

She returned her gaze to the red stoplight.

When the light turned green, she drove her demon the rest of the way home.

5

Erin turned off the car and reached for her purse in the back seat. "How will you get out of the car without opening the door? Won't the neighbors notice the door opening by itself?"

Andy tugged at the wrinkles that had developed in his suit jacket. "What kind of demon would I be if I couldn't indulge in a little sleight of hand?"

When Erin turned around, Andy was standing in front of the car with his arms folded and a smug expression on his face.

The car door on the passenger side had never opened.

She got out of the car and tried not to look at him as she walked past him and up to the front door.

Once inside, she put down her purse and let Nancy Drew out into the backyard.

Andy stuck his head in the fridge. "Shall I rustle up something for lunch?"

Before Erin could answer, there was a knock at the door.

Andy straightened up and whispered, "Who in the Nine Hells knocks in the pattern of the 'Ride of the Valkyries'?"

"My mother!" whispered Erin. "Make yourself scarce!"

Andy closed the refrigerator door and retreated to a corner of the kitchen, where he leaned against the wall with the look of someone who expects to be thoroughly entertained.

"Mom," said Erin as she opened the door. "What are you doing here?"

"That's a nice way to greet your mother," said Joyce as she crossed the threshold. "You took off like a bat out of hell. Of course I would come check on you after that!"

Andy snorted, inaudible to Joyce but perfectly noticeable by Erin.

Joyce dropped her oversized, blindingly colored cloth purse on the table and went to the refrigerator. She gazed into the interior as if it were the opening of Tut's tomb. "What is this? Some kind of science experiment?" She pulled out wilting lettuce, half-empty Tupperware, dried-up take-out, and expired milk and put it on the counter next to the fridge.

Erin rolled her eyes behind her mother's back. "Yes, Mom, that's exactly what it is."

"Don't sass me," said Joyce, without even turning around. "I can hear your eyes roll all the way over here." She closed the refrigerator door. "Keep this up, and the next thing you know, you'll be eating Nancy's dog biscuits."

Erin pressed her lips together. How did her mother know these things?

Nancy Drew doddered into the kitchen from the backyard. She raised her nose in the air and sniffed, then walked daintily over to the demon hidden in the corner and looked up expectantly.

Andy frantically shooed her away, to no avail.

To all appearances, the dog appeared to be staring raptly into a corner.

"Even your dog is acting weird," said Joyce.

Erin lunged for the dog treats. "Here, girl."

Nancy looked from Erin to Andy and back again, then turned and trotted dutifully over to Erin's general vicinity.

Erin gave her the treat and suppressed a sigh of relief.

"You feed that dog but you're not feeding yourself. When was the last time you went grocery shopping?"

"I don't know."

Andy looked back and forth between mother and daughter like a cat at a tennis match.

"When was the last time you went out with your friends?"

"I don't have any anymore."

"Don't say that," said Joyce. "Just because Genevieve—"

"I don't want to talk about it," said Erin in a warning tone.

"You can't just—"

"I said I don't want to talk about it!"

Joyce subsided into silence and bent down to stroke Nancy's silky head.

"I know you mean well, Mom. But I feel like I've been broken into a million pieces. I'm still trying to pick them all up."

Erin's mother straightened. "Can I bring you some food? A casserole?"

"It's a divorce, not a funeral. No need for covered dishes. I'll be fine. I'll go shopping, I promise."

Joyce hoisted her purse from the table onto her shoulder. She reached around Erin's shoulders and embraced her with one arm. "You'll be okay, pumpkin."

Erin didn't say anything. She didn't trust her voice not to wobble, so she nodded and walked her mother to the door instead, then watched her bustle down the driveway.

"I'll call you!" said Joyce as she stood next to the open door of her car.

Erin waved, then shut and locked the front door.

Andy leaned against the kitchen counter. "Your mom is"—he gestured vaguely as if gathering the words in mid-air—"really something."

"Tell me about it," said Erin.

"She's not entirely wrong, though."

"Don't tell me you're on her side," said Erin. She sat down at the kitchen table.

"No, no," Andy said. He came around behind her and picked up the shoulder massage where he had left off.

"Because I can't tolerate that," said Erin, closing her eyes.

"Of course not," he said, unfurling the new knots in her shoulders.

"Mmm," said Erin, half mollified and half suspicious.

"Although you really should eat better."

Erin sat bolt upright. "I knew it. You're on her side."

"No! I just think you deserve good food, that's all." He bore down more firmly and she relaxed again.

"I like food," she murmured absently.

"Why don't we go grocery shopping?"

"I don't like grocery shopping. It's tedious." Even to herself she sounded petulant. She tried for practicality. "And expensive. On my salary, at least."

"Well, I have a little rainy day money saved up. It's the least I can do if I'm taking up space." He rubbed her temples in circles.

"Come on, live a little. Don't let Mark and Genevieve have all the fun."

"That's a low blow," said Erin.

"I'm a demon; it's what I do." He pressed softly into the joint between her cheekbone and her ear.

"Ah," said Erin, tipping her head back slightly.

"Was that a yes?"

She opened her eyes, looked at his face, and knew that he knew—he'd already won the argument.

6

Andy insisted on driving halfway across town to the fancy grocery store instead of going to the perfectly good discount warehouse store around the corner.

"I fail to see how organic strawberries fit into the whole revenge thing," Erin said quietly as she piloted the cart through the produce section. She had agreed to add the items he pointed out, while he remained invisible to the other shoppers.

"Living well is the best revenge," said Andy as he pointed to a particularly juicy cluster of seedless red grapes.

She picked it up and placed it in the cart.

They reached the seafood counter. Gleaming cases packed with clear ice stretched in both directions. Inside, piles of shrimp, crab, and mussels glistened. At the far end of the counter, live lobsters with rubber bands around their claws floated in a special tank.

"Lobster," he mused. "Lots of lobster." Andy leaned down and peered into the tank. "He's a lively one," he said, indicating a

"Come on, live a little. Don't let Mark and Genevieve have all the fun."

"That's a low blow," said Erin.

"I'm a demon; it's what I do." He pressed softly into the joint between her cheekbone and her ear.

"Ah," said Erin, tipping her head back slightly.

"Was that a yes?"

She opened her eyes, looked at his face, and knew that he knew—he'd already won the argument.

6

Andy insisted on driving halfway across town to the fancy grocery store instead of going to the perfectly good discount warehouse store around the corner.

"I fail to see how organic strawberries fit into the whole revenge thing," Erin said quietly as she piloted the cart through the produce section. She had agreed to add the items he pointed out, while he remained invisible to the other shoppers.

"Living well is the best revenge," said Andy as he pointed to a particularly juicy cluster of seedless red grapes.

She picked it up and placed it in the cart.

They reached the seafood counter. Gleaming cases packed with clear ice stretched in both directions. Inside, piles of shrimp, crab, and mussels glistened. At the far end of the counter, live lobsters with rubber bands around their claws floated in a special tank.

"Lobster," he mused. "Lots of lobster." Andy leaned down and peered into the tank. "He's a lively one," he said, indicating a large lobster currently waving its claws in a particularly vigorous manner. He looked to Erin for approval.

Erin felt a little sick.

Andy peered at her. "Does this bother you? The live lobster thing?"

"It's fine," she said, barely moving her lips.

He stepped uncomfortably close, so close she could see the tiny garnet-colored flecks in his brown eyes, and looked into her eyes. "No, it isn't. How long has this bothered you?"

She shrugged and looked away.

"A while, then. While you were married to Mark?"

Erin nodded.

"You didn't like eating meat, but you kept eating it? Why?" He tapped his bearded chin. "You kept eating it because Mark did. Because you didn't want something else to come between you."

"It doesn't matter now."

"Like Hell it does. Come on." He strode through the produce department before blazing a trail through the rest of the store, pointing out fresh collard greens, grass-fed butter, black-eyed peas, vegetable broth, new crop long-grain rice, aged cheddar, and hard apple cider, along with a handful of pantry staples.

She pushed the cart in his wake, a little self-conscious but full of curiosity, loading each item into the cart.

"All vegetarian, all delicious," he said. "I'm beginning to dislike this 'Mark' character. In fact, I'm beginning to think he got off easy this morning." A faraway look came into his eyes.

If getting your trousers removed in church was getting off easy, what would be the alternative?

Erin shuddered with a mixture of fear and secret glee.

When they arrived home, he allowed her to carry in the groceries out of necessity, but after that, he sent her off straight away, insisting that he didn't need help in the kitchen and suggesting that she take a nice, long bubble bath.

Who was she to argue with a Great Earl of Hell?

Erin sank a little deeper into the bubble bath and listened to the cheery sound of pots and pans rattling in the kitchen.

Come to think of it, she'd had far more to argue about with Mark—even before the affair—than with a demon.

That didn't say much for her marriage.

Then again, perhaps that wasn't fair to Mark.

Perhaps—and this was a new and surprising thought—she didn't care. Erin turned this thought over in her mind as she idly scooped up handfuls of bubbles.

Andromalius. It had a nice ring to it. She silently formed the word with her lips, drawing out each syllable. Did he have a last name?

Would he like one?

She reached for a cup and sluiced water through her hair.

Maybe revenge could take a little longer, after all. Surely there wasn't any rush.

"Erin?" called Andy. "Dinner will be ready in twenty."

"Okay," she called through the bathroom door.

Erin pressed the lever to drain the tub, then stood up and reached for a large bath towel. She wrapped herself securely and opened the door into the master bedroom. The door from the master bedroom into the kitchen and dining area stood ajar.

"Ah, the water sprite emerges!" Andy, who had apparently borrowed one of her aprons, quickly wiped his hands and approached the bedroom. He had removed his red jacket and rolled up his crisp shirtsleeves. "Take your time," he said, keeping his gaze averted as he pulled the door closed for her.

She turned the lock out of habit and let the towel fall to the floor. She picked up a long-neglected bottle of moisturizing oil and held it in her hands for a long moment before twisting the cap free. She spread the oil over her body, working it into her elbows, knees, and feet, then reached for a small bottle of perfume. A few dabs on her wrists, behind her ears, and on the backs of her knees sent the fresh scent winging through the room.

She put on the little black dress she'd rejected that morning.

Her hair, wet but no longer dripping, responded favorably to a wide-toothed comb, leaving it damp but shining and sleek.

Erin considered the makeup arrayed on her vanity table. Her hand skipped from one lipstick tube to another, flipping them upside-down to read the tiny labels until she found the one marked "Temptation" and swiped it on her lips with a steady hand.

It was exactly the shade of Andy's red suit.

She padded barefoot across the carpet, unlocked the door, and emerged into the dining room.

Andy carefully laid the last of the feast on the dining room table. "Madam, may I present: seasoned apple cider collard greens and black-eyed peas over rice, accompanied by herbed cheddar biscuits and butter, paired with a crisp apple cider."

Erin took in the sight of the beautifully laid table, complete with lit candles, and wondered how long it had been since she felt truly cared for.

He pulled out a chair for her.

She lowered herself into it. "Thank you," she said, unable to muster the composure to add anything more elaborate.

Andy beamed. "My pleasure. Let's eat!" He seated himself across from her and filled her plate from the serving dishes. "Good nutrition, that's what you need."

Erin smiled. "Where did you learn to cook?"

"Oh, you know. Around."

"You're too modest."

"It's my great failing as a demon. I should be far more boastful." He shook his head ruefully.

They ate the vegetarian feast in silence for a few minutes.

"So, I was thinking about the whole revenge thing," said Erin.

Andy laid down his fork and gave her his full attention.

"I was thinking," Erin continued, "that if we really thought things out, we could come up with something special. Artistic, even."

Andy's eyes shone in the candlelight. "Great minds think alike. Today's activities could be just an"—he paused to search for the right word—"*amuse-bouche*, wouldn't you say?"

"Yes," said Erin, nodding solemnly and trying to look like she understood the French-sounding phrase he had just uttered. "That."

"I couldn't agree more," said Andy, helping himself to another biscuit.

She watched him take a hearty bite. "But I do have to go in to work tomorrow."

He swallowed. "And I don't even know what you do for a living! Tell me all about it while I refill your glass." He retrieved the cider and topped up both glasses.

"I'm a teacher," she said.

"Oh, wow. Of small children? Miniature mortals?"

"Yes, the miniature ones. School's not actually in session right now, but I got moved to a different grade level, so I was going to go in and get some of my stuff moved to my new classroom."

"You want a hand?" He sipped from his glass.

"I'm...not sure I could explain you. And if my boxes started carrying themselves through the school, well—it might attract attention."

"True, true."

"And you could use the time to think up lots and lots of ideas for revenge on Mark. You know, make a long list. Really long."

"There's the wickedness I was looking for. I can see it now. And I like it," he said, looking her up and down with approval.

Her stomach did a little flip. She might be out of her depth, but she'd be damned if she wasn't going to enjoy the swim.

7

Erin drove to school feeling as if something heavy had been lifted off her shoulders that she'd been carrying for a long time without ever noticing the weight—until it was gone.

She'd found Andy in the kitchen when she emerged from the bedroom in the morning. He'd greeted her warmly, handed her a cup of coffee, and returned to the table where he'd already amassed a pile of pens and stacks of scribbled-on paper.

As she turned into the school parking lot, she reflected on the fact that he'd taken what she'd said quite seriously. It was a heady sensation to be listened to. Out of habit, she flipped down the driver's side sunshade and checked her appearance. She couldn't help smiling at her own reflection.

What was happening to her?

Erin closed the mirror and stepped out of the car into the summer sunlight. It was already hot and would get hotter.

There were barely any cars in the parking lot. Most teachers, Erin included, took as much advantage as they could of their time away from school. It was too easy to burn out if you didn't take time to recharge.

Her footsteps echoed in the empty outdoor hallways. She unlocked her old classroom door and stepped into the musty air of the closed-up room. There was so much to move: boxes, computers, books, and stacks upon stacks of files.

She sighed, which turned into a cough thanks to the dust, and decided to see if the school library was unlocked. She could snag a big rolling cart if she was lucky.

It looked dark inside, which wasn't promising, and the door didn't budge despite a hard tug. She peered through the window and banged hopefully on the door. Just as she was about to turn away, she heard a voice calling from the depths of the building.

"Hang on, I'm coming!"

A woman pushed open the door from the inside. She wore a black t-shirt with the words, "Come to the Dark Side, We Have Cookies," emblazoned across the front over a pair of indigo jeans. Her frizzy hair escaped a messy bun held precariously in place by an old stick with a crystal stuck to the end. She looked over her stylish tortoiseshell glasses at Erin. "What are you doing here?"

"Hey, Raya," said Erin. "I just came in to start moving my classroom."

"Fair enough. Need a cart?"

"Yeah, a big cart would be great."

Erin entered the library. Its soaring ceilings disappeared into darkness. A desk lamp and computer provided the only illumination. Erin's eyes slowly adjusted as she followed Raya to a back room.

"So, what have you been up to this summer?" asked Raya. She turned on the back room lights.

Erin mentally flipped through an assortment of responses and discarded all of them. "Not much."

Raya began rolling smaller carts out of the way to get to a larger cart. "Not much? You either need to get out more—or you're leaving out the good stuff."

"Actually," said Erin, "I made a new friend." Raya was more of a work friend than a best friend, but it felt good to open up to someone, and Raya had always been insightful, if a bit unorthodox.

Raya froze in mid-roll and looked over her shoulder at Erin. "What?"

Erin nodded.

"Is this 'friend' of the gentleman persuasion?"

Erin nodded again.

"You're not on the rebound already, are you?"

Erin raised her eyebrows. "Why would you say that?"

Raya chuckled as she pushed a cart over to Erin. "I don't know."

"After what Mark did, I'm not exactly eager to get mixed up with someone new," said Erin.

"You want me to take care of him? I know swamps where his body will never be found." She nodded sagely at Erin. "Except maybe by an alligator."

Erin was pretty sure Raya was joking—but with Raya, it wasn't always easy to tell. "It's okay. Really."

"All right. You just say the word." She moved the scattered carts back into place. "So what's he like, this new friend?"

Erin weighed how much to tell the quirky librarian. "He's—nice."

Raya turned off the back room lights and shut the door. "They're all nice, baby, until they're not."

They returned to the library proper and sat down in two reading chairs facing each other.

"I know," said Erin. "But he's different. Really different."

"Like, good-looking? Is he smoking hot? Because that might make it worthwhile."

Erin laughed. "Yes. No. I don't know. You're making me lose my train of thought." Erin dropped her head into her hands.

"Sorry. Go on. No, wait a second." Raya leapt up and crossed the library to her personal mini-fridge, retrieved a soda, and snagged a bag of cookies from the cabinet above the fridge. She carried the goodies back and plopped into her seat across from Erin. "Okay, go on."

"He's just a friend."

"Sure, sure. Tell me about Mr. New Hot Friend." Raya popped a cookie in her mouth and chased it with a swig of soda. "Your family know about him?"

Erin twisted her necklace and looked down at the floor. "Definitely not."

Raya grinned. "Oh, not bringing the family in on this one, huh? Damn, he must be something special."

"He wanted to help me move my classroom."

Raya sat up. "Seriously? Why isn't he here today?"

"I guess I could bring him in…"

"Hell, yeah, you will! I gotta meet this guy."

Erin ignored the tiny voice whispering that this might not be the best plan. After all, moving a whole classroom would be exceptionally difficult for one person. Andy's help would make it much easier.

"We could even have lunch together tomorrow," said Raya.

"Lunch?"

"You bet," said Raya around a mouthful of cookie. "That way I can get to know Mr. New Hot Friend, see if I think he's any good for you."

"He's not my new hot friend. And if you call him that tomorrow, I'll die. I really will."

"Okay, okay. Mr. New Hot Friend is our little secret." Raya raised her soda bottle like she was making a toast.

"He's not a secret! And he's not hot." Erin felt a blush creep over her cheeks.

Raya rolled her eyes. "Fine. He's not hot, he's not a secret, and he's definitely not a rebound." She brushed the crumbs off her hands and stood. "I gotta get back to the stacks. See you tomorrow?"

"Tomorrow," Erin agreed. It was just lunch.

What could go wrong?

8

Erin opened the front door to find the living room transformed. Andy, with a marker in each hand and one tucked behind his left ear, stood in the center of the chaos.

"You're home! Don't mind the mess. It's part of my process," he said.

Erin froze just inside the door, unable to take a single step. Papers covered the entire floor. Posters lined every open wall space. A stack of binders teetered on the coffee table.

"Oops," he said, realizing that she couldn't move. He hastily gathered up an armful to clear a path for her.

"Thanks," she said. "What is all this?"

"The Plan." He gestured grandly, waving the markers through the air. The one tucked behind his ear fell out due to the vigorous motion. He picked it up and balanced it precariously on the stack of binders.

It immediately rolled off and fell to the floor.

Nancy Drew wandered over and sniffed it, then lost interest and sat down on a stack of paper.

Erin picked her way over to the couch. "Did you even sleep last night, Andy?"

"Sleep is for mortals," he said, adding a few underlines and messy star shapes to a poster titled "CAR-RELATED MISHAPS."

"You sat up all night?"

"Something like that." He stuck a fluorescent Post-It note to a poster labeled "UNWANTED PIZZA DELIVERY."

She stretched out on the couch, put her feet up, and let her eyes close. "I guess demons don't dream," she murmured to herself, recalling the strange half-dream she'd had the night of the curse.

"Nope. But I can visit other people's," he said casually.

Erin's eyes flew open. "Really?"

"Yup." He circled an entry on the "EMBARRASSING MAIL ORDER CATALOGS" poster.

She shifted her position to look more carefully at another poster. "What are 'Food and Drink Surprises'?"

"You know. Salt in the sugar bowl. Cool Whip in the mayo jar. Then you use the mayo you took out of the jar to replace the cream in some doughnuts."

Erin nearly gagged at the thought. "That's hideous."

"Isn't it?"

"You are the Michaelangelo of mayhem."

He acknowledged the compliment with a flourish. "Thank you."

"Speaking of mayhem, it turns out that my classroom was way worse than I thought. I could use a hand tomorrow, if you're free."

He sat on the opposite end of the couch. "You don't mind if I'm seen?"

"Do you have anything else you can wear?"

Andy feigned outrage. "And abandon my signature outfit?"

"Maybe something a little less conspicuous."

"If you insist." He stood up and placed his hands on his shoulders, then ran them slowly over his chest and down his abdomen to the tops of his thighs.

Erin sat up, her gaze tracking the movement of his hands. "What are you doing?"

"Exactly what you asked."

The fabric of his jacket rippled like a tilted lenticular image, changing from deep red to a professorial brown corduroy, spreading downward until his trousers also transitioned from waist to cuff.

Erin closed her mouth, which had been hanging open. "That's…very nice. But maybe a little formal for moving boxes in ninety degree weather?"

He cocked his head at her and ran his hands down his torso again, holding eye contact the entire time. This time, his ensemble rippled into a buttoned chambray shirt tucked into artfully distressed blue jeans and a jet-black leather belt.

Erin's mouth went dry. "Nice," she croaked.

He smirked. "I'm glad you approve." He rolled up his sleeves and turned back to his posters.

She felt the urge to do something for him, since he had clearly made such an effort for her. "Are you hungry? Do demons get hungry?"

Andy chuckled. "Not as a physical need, no—but appetite is a sensation of the mind, and in that sense I have hunger to spare."

"Can I fix you something?"

"Not on your life. You've been moving boxes all day. Lie down. I'll get us something."

"No, really, I don't mind." Erin started up from the couch.

He whirled around and stared her down. "Sit, mortal, before you overexert yourself."

"I don't know whether to be insulted or grateful," said Erin.

"As you please," he said with a shrug. "As long as you stay put." He left the living room for the kitchen.

She lay back and listened to the pleasantly domestic sounds of his movements.

"Do you have a tray?" he called.

"In the cabinet on the lower right."

She heard the cabinet door opening and the rasp of the tray being extracted, followed by a thump.

"Got it—oh."

"What is it?"

"Something fell out of the cabinet. No big deal."

Erin jumped off the couch and ran to the kitchen with Nancy Drew belatedly skittering in her wake. She walked in to find Andy closing a white, heavily decorated, oversized photo album.

He shoved it back in the cabinet and quickly slammed the cabinet closed. "See? No big deal."

"You saw it," she said.

He stood up and fussed with the fruit on the cutting board. "Saw what?"

"For a demon, you're a terrible liar."

Andy loaded the food onto the tray and carried it into the living room without saying anything. He set the tray on the coffee table and sat on the couch without making eye contact.

She followed him and sat on the couch next to him. "It's okay." She caught his gaze with her own. "You can talk about it. It's not like I haven't seen it before."

"That was your wedding photo album," he said.

"It was," said Erin.

"That woman. Next to you. In your wedding photos. She was at the church yesterday."

"She was."

"She was sitting with your ex-husband at church."

Erin nodded.

"That was Genevieve? One of your bridesmaids?"

Erin nodded again.

"Your friend?"

"Not anymore."

Andy picked up Nancy Drew, who had followed them into the living room, and held her close. "I'm sorry."

"Don't be."

"Was she your—best friend?" he asked.

"I thought so at the time," said Erin.

"Oh, Hell," said Andy. He gently patted Nancy Drew, his hands gliding over her furry back. "Would you like me to make all her hair fall out?"

Erin made a noise like a cross between a sob and a laugh.

"Sign her up on a hundred telemarketing lists?"

"No," Erin said. She couldn't help giggling.

"Come on, work with me. Even Nancy wants to help," he said, holding Nancy Drew up.

Nancy looked about as helpful as a small elderly dog could look.

"I don't know," said Erin, sounding doubtful. "Mosquitoes? She hates mosquitoes."

"See, I knew you could do it!"

Erin managed a half-smile. "It shouldn't bother me so much. But sometimes it's hard to stop thinking about it. I can't even escape it in my sleep."

"You dream about it?" asked Andy.

"All the time. Like a broken record."

Andy carefully set Nancy Drew down. "That's unfortunate."

"Tell me about it." Erin plucked a strawberry from the tray and took a bite.

"Have you ever tried lucid dreaming?"

Erin swallowed the bite of strawberry. "What's lucid dreaming?"

"Lucid dreaming is when you become aware that you're dreaming. Sometimes, you can even control your dreams."

"What good would that do?" She selected a piece of cheese to follow the strawberry.

Andy's eyes lit up. "Let's see. Well, instead of being tormented by scenes of the past, you could find yourself equipped with an armload of tomatoes to throw at anyone who displeased you in the dream. Or you could just banish them from the dream entirely."

Erin laughed. "That sounds fun. I can't imagine being able to do that, though."

"Maybe I can help."

His last statement, so casually delivered, hung in the air like a promise.

9

That night, Erin pulled on her pajamas and stepped into her slippers. The red wine had disappeared in the wash. She folded down one side of the bed and fluffed her pillow before dimming the lights in the room, leaving the bathroom light on and the door ajar for a trickle of illumination.

She found Andy on the other side of the house. He sat on the floor of the spare bedroom surrounded by stacks of books he had collected from around the house.

"Hey," said Erin.

Andy lowered the book he was reading—*The Screwtape Letters*—and looked up. "Hey." He placed the book on a stack and stood up gracefully.

"I was going to turn in."

He approached her softly, as if she were a deer and likely to bolt. "Are you sure about this?"

Erin nodded. "I'm sure."

"It can be a little strange, going lucid for the first time."

"I can imagine. But I'm willing to try anything." Erin paused. "How will you do it?"

"Do what?"

"How will you enter my dreams? What happens?"

"When you're fast asleep and dreaming, I'll know. Then I'll close my eyes and follow you into the dream. I think it's not unlike what mortals call meditation." He laid his hand on her cheek as if he were soothing a fevered child. "You'll see me as a natural part of your dream."

"Will you have to be in the room with me?"

He lowered his hand. "Being nearby is good enough."

"That's good," said Erin. "I'm not sure I could fall asleep with someone staring at me."

Andy chuckled. "Goodnight, Erin."

"Goodnight, Andy."

Erin returned to her bedroom alone, oddly aware of Andy's presence even though he was on the other side of the house. She crawled into the bed and drew the covers up.

Falling asleep had been difficult for a long time. Waiting for a demon to show up in her dreams should have made it worse. In a way, the anticipation did make it hard to fall asleep, somewhat like trying to fall asleep the night before a big vacation. Still, it was a far better sensation than the angst-filled nights of tossing and turning and going over every terrible event in her mind until she dropped, exhausted, into a sleep filled with torturous dreams.

She rolled over and sighed. Random images flitted through her mind.

The bed, the room, and the world around faded from her awareness.

She found herself standing alone in the living room of the darkened house. She shivered.

Andy's voice floated over her shoulder. "Erin," he said.

Erin turned to look for him. "Andy?"

He appeared out of the darkness, a faint corona of red highlighting him all the way around, even to the tips of his wings, which he extended to full length before folding them behind him like an eagle. "Do you remember? You're dreaming now."

"But it feels so real," said Erin. She looked around and realized that beyond the living room, the scene faded into utter blackness. "This is really weird."

"Do you want to wake up?"

"No!" Erin placed her hand on his arm. "Not yet. What happens next, though?"

Andy shrugged. "That's up to you. And your subconscious mind."

Erin patted herself. "If I'm here, how am I separate from my subconscious?"

"You're dreaming lucidly now. You're in a dream, but you're aware of it."

"Okay." She looked out the window of her dream-house. The light outside went from nonexistent to full sun in the blink of an eye. She watched as Mark's car pulled into the driveway.

The dream flickered. Mark stood in the kitchen. No; it wasn't Mark—it was a dream-Mark.

A dream-Erin walked into the kitchen.

This was how it always started.

Erin and Andy watched the scene unfold.

"Where were you?" said dream-Erin.

"I had to work late," said dream-Mark. "Lots to do."

"You're always working late these days."

"So? You don't want me to be successful?"

"Of course I want you to be successful. But we hardly see each other any more, Mark. I'm lonely."

Mark took a sports drink out of the refrigerator and twisted the cap off. "Oh? Is that a threat? Are you threatening to find someone else?"

"That's ridiculous! How can you even say that?"

"Well, with you acting so weird, what am I supposed to think?" He guzzled the drink and dropped the empty container on the kitchen counter with more force than necessary.

The dream flickered again. The Mark and Erin of the dream disappeared, and the sunlight died, leaving the house in silent darkness.

"You okay?" said Andy.

"Yeah," said Erin. "I dream about that all the time. It's surreal to watch from the outside, though."

The walls around them shifted and re-formed to reveal the interior of a chain coffee shop, decorated with dark wood and accented with sleek fixtures in stylish neutral tones.

"This is definitely a nightmare," said Andy. "This place has the worst coffee in the world."

"What is it with you and your coffee snobbery?"

"I'm naturally judgmental." He winked at her and ruffled his wings.

"Oh, no," said Erin.

"What?" He followed her gaze across the coffee shop.

"It's me again."

Andy stared. "And Genevieve."

Erin's face hardened.

Dream-Genevieve, with long blonde hair trailing over the back of her chair, sat with her back to them, deep in conversation with dream-Erin at a table for two. Their words became audible as if someone had suddenly turned up the volume of their voices.

"I don't know, Genny. Something's just not right."

"Don't overthink it." Dream-Genevieve sipped from her mocha shake drizzled in ribbons of caramel, then paused to wipe some whipped cream from the tip of her nose. "He's just busy."

"I guess…"

"He just wants to earn more money. Is that so bad?" Dream-Genevieve gazed across the coffee shop rather than make eye contact with Dream-Erin.

"I guess not. But he doesn't seem too happy with me right now, either."

"I'm sure it'll be fine," Dream-Genevieve said, looking down into her drink, which had rapidly dissolved into an unappetizing mess.

The room likewise dissolved, returning Erin and Andy to the darkened dream-house where they'd started.

"Damn it," said Erin. "No matter how many times I relive that stupid conversation, I can't believe I bought it. She was lying to me the whole time—and I trusted her. Like an idiot." She rubbed her hands across her forehead. "She had been cheating with him for months at that point."

"Would it help to cancel all her credit cards and hide a fish in her car?"

Erin sighed. "I don't even know."

Andy patted her back. "Just say the word and she'll get a box of unlabeled chocolate covered ants mailed right to her door. From Mark."

Erin snorted. "Not that she needs extra chocolate presents. She's the one in a relationship right now. You could send me some."

"I would never send you chocolate covered ants."

"What kind of chocolates would you send me?"

Andy's red outline of light deepened in color.

"Are you blushing?" said Erin. "Is that how demons blush?" Why would he blush, anyway?

"I wasn't blushing. I was just thinking." Andy attempted to glower at her.

He wasn't good at glowering. Erin laughed so hard she had to grab on to Andy for support to keep from toppling over.

"This is what I get for living around mortals for a few thousand years," he muttered to himself. "Hang-ups. I should have minded my business and stayed out of trouble, but no—I was 'bored' and 'needed something to do.'" His fingers shaped the air quotes, which hung in space like afterimages before fading into darkness.

Erin batted her eyelashes at the flustered demon. "You're not having fun?"

He looked her up and down. "All right, mortal. You want chocolate? Give me your hands."

She backed up, holding her hands out of reach.

"I'm not going to bite you, Erin. Trust me."

Erin relented and placed her hands in his. Even in the dream, his hands felt unusually warm.

"Now. Think about a box of chocolate. Think about the best chocolate you've ever tasted. Imagine the pieces arrayed in a beautiful box just for you. Aren't they pretty? Like shiny, edible jewels with colorful fillings. Can you see it?"

Erin nodded.

"This is your dream. You're in control. Imagine the box."

A splendid box appeared between them, hovering in mid-air. "Take it."

Erin released Andy's hands and took the box. "How did you do that?"

Andy shook his head. "I didn't. You did. I just helped you get the hang of it."

She eagerly lifted the lid of the box. Sure enough, it brimmed with chocolate bonbons of every kind. "Can I eat them?"

"This is your dream. You can do anything you want."

Erin bit into one and felt the chocolate melt on her tongue. "It's delicious!"

He smiled. "Of course it is. You made it, after all."

"Do you want to try one?"

Her suggestion brought an adorable look of surprise to his face. "Sure, if I may."

She selected a round piece, the shape reminiscent of a chocolate-covered cherry, and held it out to him.

He took it and popped it into his mouth whole.

Without warning, light illuminated the house as if it were a stage. Lightning flickered outside, followed by the crackle of thunder.

"Oh, God—not now," said Erin, with pure dread in her voice. She closed the box and tucked it under her arm.

"What is it?"

Erin shook her head. "You'll see."

Another dream-Erin stormed into the room. "How could you do this to me? You said you loved me!"

Dream-Mark followed her. "I'm sorry, Erin. I didn't mean for this to happen."

"How can you even say that?"

"It just happened, okay?"

"Do I look stupid? Nothing 'just happens,' Mark. And with Genevieve? My best friend? For God's sake!"

"Neither of us meant to hurt you."

"That's rich!"

Dream-Mark shrugged. "I don't know what else to say to you."

"Then just leave."

He walked out the front door and disappeared into the flickering landscape outside the dream-house.

Dream-Erin seized the wedding album from its place on the coffee table and hurled it across the room. It smashed into the wall and bounced off, hitting the floor and tumbling over before coming to a stop with its pages askew. Dream-Erin collapsed to the ground and wept.

The dream-house and the dream-Erin faded into blackness.

Erin—the real Erin—woke up in her bed. She felt around for the box of chocolate, before realizing it didn't actually exist. "Andy!"

He was already standing at the foot of the bed, gray wings spread, backlit by the faint light of the rising sun. The scent of cinnamon and woodsmoke filled the room. He moved to kneel beside the bed, where he extended one wing over her, part canopy, part blanket, and she buried her face in the soft feathers until her heart rate slowed and the morning light glowed just a little brighter.

Andy slowly lifted his wing. "Are you okay? Lucid dreaming can be intense."

"I'm okay. I want my chocolate back, though."

He chuckled in obvious relief. "That's my Erin." He folded his wings out of sight. "You need a good breakfast before we move your classroom boxes." He tapped the tip of her nose with one warm finger.

"Yes, Mother." Erin sat up with a contented sigh. She couldn't help but luxuriate in his concern.

"So hop in the shower like a good mortal and I'll rustle something up."

"Yes, Mother," she said, stifling a giggle.

"And if you call me Mother one more time, you'll find out how I take revenge on foolish mortals who refuse to call me by my rightful name."

"Yes, M—Andy."

"Mandy?"

"Andy," said Erin. "Andromalius, Great Earl of Hell, Discoverer of Wickedness." She bowed to him with sarcastic panache.

"That's more like it."

She stood up and found Nancy Drew at her feet. "Great Earl of Blushing," she called as she walked into the kitchen for a glass of water, Nancy trotting behind.

"You're never going to let that go, are you?"

"Nope."

He followed her into the kitchen. "I stand by my suggestions. You can't let all these wonderful ideas go to waste." He gestured to the posters still covering the living room.

The poster titled "THINGS TO HIDE THAT WILL EVENTUALLY STINK" came unstuck on one side and swung loose to an off-kilter angle.

10

Erin, sensibly attired in comfortable clothes she didn't mind getting dusty, shut her car door and joined Andy on the sidewalk bordering the school parking lot. She allowed herself one quick observation of his appearance.

Of course, it was only to make sure that he looked completely un-demon-like.

In the full light of the morning sun, he appeared quite normal. Anyone would take him for a regular guy, albeit a regular guy with impeccable grooming, remarkable eyes, and unselfconscious charisma.

Erin shook her head to clear her thoughts. "Let's go," she said.

They walked through the deserted hallways to Erin's classroom. She unlocked the door and ushered Andy inside.

Andy looked around, taking in the posters on the wall and the assortment of dented desks in the center of the room. "Wow," he said.

"It usually looks better than this," she said.

"No, I like it," he said.

"I had to take most of my stuff down already."

He nodded. "Where do we start?"

"With these, I guess," said Erin, pointing to the jumble of desktop computers, monitors, and cables piled on one of the large, sturdy tables.

Every load they placed on the rolling cart and transported to Erin's new classroom reduced the furnishings in her old room until the only things remaining were large pieces, like storage cabinets and tables, that wouldn't be moved. By lunchtime, the only task remaining was to remove the last posters from the walls.

"I like that you're into posters, too," said Andy, carefully unsticking the corners of the classroom rules poster.

"Comes with the territory," said Erin.

"If I were a teacher, I would make so many posters."

Erin laughed. "I bet you would. I bet there wouldn't be a single square inch of wall space left."

"And if the students acted up, I would make my eyes glow red to terrify them into being good."

"Probably not the best approach."

Andy went on, caught up in the fantasy of being a demon/teacher. "And everyone would ask me how I kept my class in line, and I would just smile mysteriously."

Erin couldn't help but smile at the mental picture of Andy trying to control a bunch of misbehaving children. "Sure. And when the principal asked you why the students ran screaming out of your class, you'd have a perfectly good explanation."

Andy considered this. "Good point. Okay, no red eyes. How about giving the kids a stern lecture about the state of their souls?"

"That would not go over well."

"Damn it," said Andy. "I'm all out of options. Guess I'll have to leave the teaching to the professionals."

"That's probably for the best."

"You ready for lunch?"

"I didn't pack anything," she said. "I guess we can drive through somewhere."

"Ha! Drive through somewhere? Not on your life. I'm not going to Taco Hell or some other substandard eatery."

"Oh? Is that so? Well, then, what do you suggest, Mr. Demon Foodie?"

"Stay put. I'll be right back." He threw open the classroom door and jogged off in the direction of the parking lot.

Erin busied herself with the remaining wall decorations.

A few minutes later, Andy returned with a large wicker hamper.

Erin ran to the door and held it open for him. "What is that?"

"Just a little lunch." He set the hamper on an empty table.

"Are you serious?" She flipped open the lid and peeked inside, catching a glimpse of sandwiches, fruit, cheese, chips, cookies, and little bottles of soda.

"I put it together while you were getting ready. Do you like it?" He turned his garnet-flecked brown eyes to her, seeking her approval.

It was charming. She resisted a sudden urge to kiss his cheek.

"Of course I like it! It's lovely. Can I help you carry it?"

"Why? Are we going somewhere?"

"I promised my friend in the library that we'd meet her for lunch. She has the bigger space, so I said we'd come there."

"Any friend of yours is a friend of mine." He reached for the basket. "I'll carry this."

They walked to the library in the center of the school.

Erin pulled on the library door handle. This time, it was unlocked.

They were expected.

Erin entered the darkened library and spotted Raya sitting at her desk, facing her computer with her back to the entrance.

Andy followed, hauling the oversized basket.

"Hey, Raya," said Erin, hoping Raya remembered to refrain from calling Andy "Mr. New Hot Friend."

Raya turned in her office chair, squinting into the intrusion of the outdoor light. She took off her glasses and polished them on her t-shirt, which read "Don't Make Me Use My Librarian Voice."

"Hey, you're here," said Raya. "Who's that with you?"

"This is my friend Andy. He helped me move my classroom this morning."

"Hi, Andy." Raya stood up, still polishing her glasses, and approached Erin and Andy.

"I'm sure there's enough for three," said Andy, hefting the basket as if he were weighing it.

"I'm starving," said Raya, sliding her glasses into place. She took one look at Andy and froze.

"Raya? Where should we put this?" asked Erin.

Raya backed up a step. "You're not—" she stammered.

Andy's eyes widened as he looked Raya up and down, from her black boots to her blue jeans to her librarian t-shirt, and then up to her bun pinned in place with the gnarled stick. "Wait a minute," he said. "I can explain!"

Raya pulled the crystal-tipped stick out of her hair, unleashing a puff of frizzy curls. "Like Hell you can." Her voice shook but her arm was steady as she pointed her hair accessory at Andy.

"Raya, why are you pointing your hair stick at my friend?"

"He's not your friend," said Raya.

"Let's just all stay calm here—" said Andy.

"Put the basket down," said Raya.

Andy opened the lid. "Look, it's just sandwiches—"

"I said drop it, demon!"

Erin gasped. How could Raya know?

Andy slowly lowered the basket to the ground. He straightened and held his hands out, palms facing Raya. "Now, let's not do anything rash—"

"Demon, be gone!" Raya shouted and flicked the stick down and out toward Andy, as if she were cracking a whip.

"Raya, no!" cried Erin. She had only enough time to catch the desperate expression on Andy's face as he reached for her before he disappeared in a coruscating web of light.

He was gone.

Erin stared where Andy had just been standing, then looked at Raya. "What did you do to him?"

Raya, her chest heaving as if she had just run a marathon, pivoted to all four corners of the library with her hair stick—or, really, what could only be called her wand—fully extended before her. "Hold on. I have to make sure there aren't any more."

"Any more what? There's no one here but us!"

She faced Erin. "I think we're okay." Raya held the stick in her teeth as she wound up her hair into a bun again, then jammed the wand through the bun. "Erin, I think you need to sit down."

"I don't want to sit down! What did you do to Andy?"

"You didn't bother to tell me Mr. New Hot Friend—"

"Andy! His name is Andy!" Erin felt close to tears.

"Fine, whatever! You didn't bother to tell me Mr. New Hot Friend Andy was a demon!"

The room tilted around Erin. She reached out to a nearby chair to steady herself. "I didn't think it was important! And how did you know, anyway?"

Raya put her hands on her hips. "How long have you been hanging out with supernatural creatures?"

"Supernatural? He's just Andy. And answer the question—how did you even know he was anything out of the ordinary?"

"Sit down." Raya steered Erin into one of the library chairs and sat across from her. "What I'm about to tell you does not leave this room. Capisce?"

"What? Okay, fine, just tell me."

Raya gave her a long look before continuing. "Erin, I'm a witch."

"You're a witch?" Erin's voice rose in volume and pitch as she spoke.

"Keep your voice down. And, yes, I am," said Raya. "This isn't something I want shared on the six o'clock news, all right?"

"How can you be a witch? You're a librarian."

Raya rolled her eyes. "You think witches go around wearing pointy hats? Can you imagine what would happen if I went public with my unusual religious beliefs? I'd be fired so fast my head would spin."

Erin's newest friend was a demon. Her oldest work friend was a secret witch.

Erin's grip on reality was threatening to slip.

"But why did you zap Andy?"

"I didn't 'zap' him—I banished him. And it was for your own safety!"

"He was perfectly safe!" said Erin.

"You knew he was a demon?"

"Yes, I knew!"

"You knew he was a demon and you were hanging around with him?"

"He was helping me."

Raya scoffed and made a dismissive gesture. "Since when do demons help people?"

"This one did. He made me dinner, he helped me move my classroom, he stayed with me during my bad dreams—"

"Hold up. Your dreams? You let a demon into your dreams? Are you insane?"

"I'm not—"

"Your dreams, Erin! You let him into your mind!"

"It's not like that—"

"Look, I know you're having a hard time, but—"

"You don't understand," said Erin. "He's very sweet."

"Sure, until he corrupts you and tarnishes your soul."

"He's the only person who's been nice to me since the divorce."

"News flash, Erin: he's not a person. And isn't that exactly how a demon would take advantage of you? When you're vulnerable? Needy?"

"I'm not needy," said Erin.

"Sure you are. You just got a divorce, for God's sake. You're allowed to be needy. Vulnerable. Whatever. Just not with a demon!"

"I'll be careful," said Erin. "I promise. Just bring him back. Please?"

Raya sighed. "I can't bring your demon back."

"What do you mean, you can't? You're the one who blasted him in the first place!"

"Yeah, it's not like a two-way street. I don't specialize in conjuring demons. I just know how to get rid of 'em."

"But—he's gone? Just like that?" Erin felt sick.

Raya looked down. "I'm sorry."

Erin's mind raced. "Maybe if I cursed Mark again—"

"You cursed your ex-husband? Is that how this started?"

"It was an accident. The next thing you know, there's some odd guy in a red bow tie in my kitchen, asking me how I like my coffee and exactly what kind of revenge I want to take on Mark."

Raya gave her an appraising look. "Has anything like this ever happened to you before?"

"Never," said Erin.

"No funny dreams? No seeing things other people can't see?"

"No, why?"

"What was your demon's name, again?"

"Andy."

"That's not a very demonic name."

"It's short for Andromalius."

"Interesting," said Raya. She got up and moved the picnic basket to the table, then flipped open the lid.

"Can you please try to bring him back? He really was helping me."

Raya looked up from the basket and eyed Erin. "Did you have some kind of thing for this demon?"

"No! I mean, he was really kind to me, and he went shopping with me and fixed dinner for me and came up with these elaborate charts of things he could do to torment Mark..." Erin trailed off as the memories rushed back. "Are you sure cursing Mark again wouldn't work?"

"I doubt it. Sounds like it was a freak accident in the first place." Raya paused and retrieved a stack of sandwiches from inside of the basket. "Although you probably should be careful with what you say in the future. You might have some kind of latent ability. Anyway, what would you do if you did get your demon back? Were you really going to go through with some elaborate revenge plot?"

"I don't know," said Erin. "I didn't think he'd be gone so soon."

"Here, eat something." Raya held out a package of sandwiches to Erin.

"You think—I have some kind of ability? What ability?" Erin reached out to take the proffered sandwiches.

"Honestly, I have no idea. Don't try anything stupid, okay? Like taking matters into your own hands?" She pointed a bottle of soda at Erin.

"How would I even do that?" said Erin.

"By trying to conjure him up by yourself. God knows what you could end up with."

"What could I end up with?" asked Erin.

Raya gave her a dark look. "You don't want to know."

Determination welled up within Erin, accompanied by an impulse to do something Raya would never expect. As soon as Raya looked down and bit into one of Andy's sandwiches, Erin darted forward and snatched the wand right out of Raya's hair.

11

"What the—" Raya dropped her sandwich and jumped to her feet, knocking the basket over. "Give me that."

Erin backed away. "I'm getting my demon back and you're not going to stop me."

"You're messing with things you don't understand, Erin. Put the wand down."

"You're not giving me any choice! You won't help me!" Erin continued backing away from Raya, heading toward the exit.

"For God's sake, stop being a damned fool!" Raya stalked across the library, fury in her eyes.

Erin turned to run to the door, but made it only a few feet before Raya tackled her and sent her crashing into the thin industrial carpet over the concrete floor. The impact knocked the breath out of Erin.

With a strength she didn't know she had, Erin pushed Raya away and sprang to her feet with the wand in her hand, then ran out the door. She had no plan but to keep running until she got to her car in the parking lot. As she looked over her shoulder to see if Raya was following her, she slammed into someone rounding the corner in front of her.

"Oh, my goodness, I'm so sorry," Erin blurted. She had only an impression of a cobalt blue power suit and black leather pumps before it dawned on her who she'd run into. "So sorry—Mrs. Claiborne."

Mrs. Claiborne, the school principal and Erin's boss, was the worst possible person she could have run into at that moment.

"Erin," said Mrs. Claiborne in a cool tone that somehow conveyed both greeting and chastisement.

Erin realized she still clutched the wand in her hand. She put it behind her back. "Are you okay, Mrs. Claiborne? I'm so sorry I ran into you."

Mrs. Claiborne brushed at her suit. "I'm all in one piece. Where were you going in such a hurry?"

In her peripheral vision, Erin saw Raya emerge from the library.

"Oh, I—uh—forgot something in my car. For my new classroom. So I ran out to get it," said Erin, trying to wrap up the conversation quickly.

It was too late. Raya sauntered up to Erin and Mrs. Claiborne.

"Raya," said Mrs. Claiborne.

"Hey, Mrs. C," said Raya. "How's your summer going?"

"Fine, thank you. And yours?"

Raya casually dropped her arm around Erin's shoulders. "Absolutely great. In fact, my friend Erin and I"—she paused to aim a grin at Erin—"were just finishing up our lunch when—"

"Yes!" interrupted Erin. "When I had to go get something from the car."

"Yes," Raya drawled. "She had to get something from the car. And—look at that—Erin, did you find my lost hair stick?" She reached behind Erin and pulled the wand from Erin's unresisting hand, tucking it securely into her own pocket. "Thank you so much. I've been looking for it everywhere."

Erin could do nothing but smile even as she wanted to scream in frustration.

"Well, we should get back to it. Have a nice summer, Mrs. C," said Raya. Keeping her arm around Erin, she steered her back to the library, closed the door, and locked it.

Embarrassment mingled with Erin's despair. She faced Raya. "I'm sorry I grabbed your wand," she said. "I don't know what got into me."

"Demonic possession?"

"No, that was all me," said Erin ruefully.

"Sit down," said Raya. "Stop being crazy. I have more questions to ask you."

Erin, heavy with misery, sank into a chair.

"Did this demon have some kind of control over you?"

"I—" Erin swallowed and considered her next words. "No. I don't think so. He—it was more like he did what I wanted."

"He was helping you."

"With a lot of things." She didn't elaborate the point because she didn't trust herself not to start crying on the spot. "Why?"

"Okay. I'm going to overlook the fact that you nearly got me in big trouble with the boss—"

Erin wanted to disappear on the spot. Instead, she briefly covered her face with her hands. "I'm so sorry. I panicked."

Raya waved away the apology. "I shouldn't have jumped to conclusions about Mr. New Hot Friend. He is pretty hot, by the way."

Erin couldn't help but smile, just a little.

Raya continued. "You seem to have some kind of—I don't know—something. Otherwise you wouldn't have been able to call him up in the first place. Maybe we can figure this out. If we work together."

Erin sat forward in her chair. "Can we try to call him up now?"

"What, now? You think it's a good idea to do that in the middle of my library?" said Raya, helping herself to more goodies from the basket.

"It's not?" said Erin.

"You mean besides the whole getting-fired-for-witchcraft-at-work thing? No way." She bit into a sandwich. "We'll go to my house later."

12

Erin sped home with the empty picnic basket in the backseat and Raya's rather unusual shopping list tucked into her purse. As she drove down her street, she spotted a car in her driveway.

It was her mother, of course. Never content with a phone call, Joyce would turn up on her doorstep at any hour of the day.

Erin parked the car and got out. "Hi, Mom," she said as her mother exited her large sedan.

"Were you at school, darling? Did you move your classroom all by yourself?"

White lies were often easier than the unvarnished truth. "Yup," said Erin, unlocking the front door and letting her mother precede her into the house.

As she stepped inside, Erin's stomach dropped. She'd forgotten Andy's handiwork. "Mom, can you let Nancy out?" She stepped between her mother and the living room.

"Sure," said Joyce. She headed for the kitchen.

Erin exhaled and ran to the living room, frantically pulling down poster after poster, each one with more dire revenge ideas than the last. She wrestled the pile of posters into the hall closet and slammed the door.

"Is that you, Erin? Do you need help?" called her mother.

"Just putting something away, Mom." Erin went to the kitchen, dropped her purse on the table, and found her mother peering in the refrigerator. Again.

"This is much better. You have actual food in here. What is this?" Joyce picked up the container of leftovers.

"Just some rice and beans with greens."

"You'll have to give me the recipe," said her mother, closing the refrigerator.

"Absolutely," said Erin. "I'll do that." Would her mother still want the recipe if she knew its demonic origin? Best not to find out. "Oh, look, here comes Nancy Drew." She slid open the patio door to allow the dog to enter, then gave Nancy a dog treat.

"She'll get fat if you keep feeding her treats, Erin."

"She's fine, Mom," said Erin, squatting to pat Nancy.

"What's this?" said Joyce. She plucked out a piece of paper that was sticking out of Erin's purse.

"Nothing." Erin stood up quickly and attempted to grab the paper.

Joyce blocked her and deftly put on her reading glasses. "Let's see. Candles, matchsticks."

"Mom—"

"Hold your horses. I'm not done." She continued reading the list. "Cinnamon sticks. Sandalwood. Garlic. Rose petals, ginger, and kosher salt. Cayenne pepper and licorice? What on earth?"

"It's a recipe," said Erin, who used her mother's temporary confusion to snatch the paper back.

"A recipe for what?"

Erin thought fast. "Bath stuff."

"With garlic and cayenne pepper?" Her mother made a face.

"I mean, some of it's bath stuff. The rest is for cooking."

"Right…" Joyce looked Erin up and down. "Are you okay?"

"I'm fine."

"Don't get testy," said her mother.

"I'm not testy," said Erin. "I'm fine."

Joyce snorted and walked into the living room.

Erin followed her. "Why don't you believe me?"

Her mother sat down on the couch and draped her arm over the back. "I—" She made a funny face and shifted her arm to feel down the back of the couch. She pulled a large poster up from behind the couch where it had fallen.

Erin's eyes widened as the poster titled "THINGS TO HIDE THAT WILL EVENTUALLY STINK" emerged.

Joyce read the poster aloud with increasing disbelief in her voice. "Tuna fish in the curtain rods, blue cheese in the couch cushions, eggs in the car, shrimp in the toilet tank, ground beef under the doormat? Erin, what is this?" She gestured at the poster.

"I was just brainstorming for a game."

Her mother peered at the poster. "But this isn't your handwriting."

Erin opened her mouth but nothing came out.

"Did you have a friend over?" Joyce gasped and put her hand to her chest. "A man friend?"

"Mom!"

"Are you dating? Did he—" Joyce's eyes opened wide as the realization hit her. "Did he make the food in the refrigerator?"

"Why would you say that?"

"Well, it's not like you're much of a cook."

"Thanks a lot."

Joyce settled back on the couch. "So, tell me everything!"

"There's nothing to tell. Sorry to disappoint you, Mom, but no, I'm not seeing, dating, or cooking with any man." Andy was a demon, she reasoned, and didn't count.

Joyce let out a long sigh. "Is old Mark holding you back, honey?"

"Mom! First you're telling me to get back together with him, next you're calling him 'Old Mark' and grilling me about my new man-friend. Make up your mind."

"I just want you to be happy."

"I am happy."

"Maybe you should find some new friends."

"I had lunch with my work friend, Raya, today." Erin left out the part about magic wands and demon-banishing.

"See? That's lovely."

Erin didn't correct her. "In fact, she's the one who made that poster."

"Why didn't you say so?"

"I didn't want you to think she was crazy, or something."

"Instead you wanted me to think you were crazy?"

Erin shrugged, unable to come up with an improvement on her spontaneous fabrication.

"I'm sure she's very nice. Why don't you invite her to church some time?"

Erin's polite smile nearly slipped. "I think she already has a church." A church with pentagrams instead of crosses, perhaps, but a religious institution all the same.

"Oh, well."

After a pause, Erin spoke. "Did you come here for any particular reason, Mom?"

"Yes. Yes, I did. I came to talk to you about something. Are you comfortable?"

Anxiety prickled over Erin. "Yes, I'm comfortable. Why? You act like I need to be sitting down for this."

"Genevieve has moved in with Mark."

"Already?"

Her mother nodded. "I can't condone it, but young people today…" She shrugged. "What can you do? Anyway, I thought you should hear it from me first."

"Thanks, I guess."

"You guess?"

"I'm glad I heard it from you, and not some gossipmonger." This elided the fact that her mother was an inveterate gossipmonger.

"I know you were working so hard to remodel Mark's house when all that went down. Those granite countertops—"

"I'm just glad my little old house hadn't sold yet. At least I had someplace to go," said Erin with false cheer.

"This is a nice little house," said her mother, in the way that a parent says something just to make you feel better.

"Granite countertops aren't all they're cracked up to be," said Erin.

Joyce leaned in and patted Erin's knee. "Neither was Mark," she said.

13

The night that she was supposed to visit Raya's house, Erin couldn't stop putting her nervous energy into straightening the couch cushions and other pointless activities.

Nancy Drew, who had followed her hopefully around the kitchen as she wiped down the counters a second time, finally gave up and sat down on the tile nearest the treat jar just in case.

Erin packed up all the items on Raya's list and sat down at the kitchen table to watch the clock. When it was reasonably close to the appointed time—she'd only be 15 minutes early—Erin sprang up, ran out the door, and jumped in the car.

She managed to drive only ten miles per hour over the speed limit on her way there.

Upon arriving at Raya's normal-looking house—except for the jaunty "Trespassers Will Be Cursed" sign—Erin knocked on the door. She'd picked up her mother's habit of knocking to the rhythm of the "Ride of the Valkyries."

The door opened.

"Well, hello there," said Raya, wearing her typical jeans and t-shirt combo. Tonight's t-shirt read "Something Wicked This Way Comes."

"Hi," said Erin, feeling a bit shy. She'd never been to Raya's house before.

Raya threw the door open wide. "Come on in. Pardon the mess!"

Erin had one foot over the threshold when a large black dog with a white spot on its chest gallumphed over and headbutted her leg.

"Sorry about the dog," said Raya. To the dog, she said, "Blaze! Get off, you dumb dog."

The dog ignored her and leaned harder against Erin, nearly bowling her over.

"Well, hello there to you, too," said Erin, attempting to pat the dog while also pushing it back into an upright position.

"All right, you." Raya coaxed the muscular animal down a hallway and behind a flimsy-looking dog gate.

"Will that hold him?"

"Her. Blaze is a she."

"She looks like she could eat that gate for breakfast."

"Probably. She's a real sweetheart, but she doesn't know her own strength."

Erin had no idea whether to nod politely or laugh. Instead, she watched Blaze chase her own tail in circles behind the gate.

"Anyway, come on through. We're all set up in the kitchen."

"Set up?"

"Yeah. For the spell?"

"Oh! Right."

"I can't wait to actually meet this demon," said Raya. "He sounds like a real character."

In the kitchen, Erin looked around for a place to set her bag of supplies, but every square inch was full.

Raya swept her arm through the jumble of candles, rocks, papers, small glass jars half full of unknown powders, and plant clippings in varying states of freshness. "Just put it up there."

Erin complied. "How does it work? The spell, that is," said Erin.

"It's like a recipe, really. Not all that different from what you'd see in a cookbook. Except instead of ending up with a pan of brownies, you get a demon." She pulled Erin's purchases out of the bag, inspecting each one before setting it aside.

"I guess I expected it to be more complicated somehow."

Raya shrugged. "Oh, complications happen. Just like with recipes. You can't always predict the result. There's an element of luck on top of the element of skill." She seized the container of salt and ripped it open. "Back up a second."

Erin backed up.

Raya drizzled a stream of salt in a swooping pattern on the linoleum floor, then layered sweet-smelling items over the salt and set aside the more pungent items, like licorice and garlic.

"What are those for?" Erin peered over Raya's shoulder.

"Sweet stuff to draw him in. Not-so-sweet stuff in case we need to get rid of something less— shall we say—friendly."

"Less friendly?" Erin's mouth went dry and she swallowed involuntarily.

"You never know," said Raya.

"Are you sure this is safe?"

Raya laughed. "Of course it's not 'safe.' Nothing's 'safe.' What, you want to live forever?" She shot Erin a crooked grin.

"Maybe not forever, but a normal lifespan would be nice."

"You want this demon back, or not?"

Erin squared her shoulders. "I want him back."

"Then let's do this." She kneeled and returned to the intricate work of decorating the salt design with rose petals at precise intervals.

Erin looked out the window. The harsh light of the sun softened as it slid closer to the horizon. "Shouldn't we be doing this at midnight or something?"

"Nah," said Raya. "Sunrise and sunset are in-between times. Good for reaching out to things that are neither here nor there." She stood up and dusted off her hands. "And that's where we find your guy."

"He's not my—"

"Whatever. You ready?"

Erin nodded.

From down the hallway, Blaze barked.

Raya lit candles and placed them around the design on the floor.

"Should I turn out the lights?" said Erin.

Raya nodded.

Erin flipped the switches and stood next to Raya.

Raya closed her eyes and murmured words that Erin couldn't quite catch. She tugged her wand free from her hair and held it over the design, then spoke clearly. "We summon the demon known as Andromalius."

Nothing happened.

Raya opened her eyes. "Hold my hand."

Erin obediently placed her hand in Raya's free hand.

"Say his name with me on the count of three. One, two, three."

"Andromalius!"

There was a banging sound from down the hall.

Something like faint smoke rose from the salt.

Erin and Raya backpedaled away from the design as a shadowy form coalesced in the center.

A silhouette of feathered wings bloomed from within the confines—except these wings weren't gray. They were the precise deep crimson shade of red velvet cake.

"Andy?" Erin squinted into the shadows.

The red-winged figure pivoted to face them. His three piece suit shone softly in the light of the candles, and he clutched a bottle of champagne in one hand, and two flutes in the other.

"What do you lot want?" he asked, his English accent dripping annoyance from every vowel and consonant.

"Where's Andromalius?" said Erin.

His lips twisted. "How the Hell should I know?"

Raya stepped closer, wand extended. "Listen, demon, we're looking for one of your friends. Andromalius. Goes by Andy. Ever heard of him?"

He rolled his eyes. "Listen, sweetheart, I don't have time for your little witch games. I was in the middle of a very nice party when I was rudely interrupted by—"

"Little witch games? I'll blast your stupid demon face straight to—"

Erin placed a restraining hand on Raya's arm. "What my friend here was trying to say was that we really need to find Andromalius. Can you please help us?"

The red-winged demon leaned closer to Erin. "What's in it for me, then?"

"I—I don't know," stammered Erin.

"Oh, just let me blast him," said Raya.

"No! Wait. Listen, demon. I'm not trying to scare you, but I've seen this woman"—she indicated Raya—"with my very own eyes, blast a demon right out of this world."

He eyed Raya with one eyebrow raised. "Really."

Erin nodded vigorously. "Poof. Gone. And I'd really hate for that to happen to you."

Phoenix looked back and forth between them. "What is this, some kind of good witch, bad witch routine?"

"Not at all," said Erin. "I just think we can work this out to everyone's mutual benefit."

"Really? Well, let me tell you something," he said. "I don't appreciate being threatened by jumped-up mortal witches who want me to be their errand boy."

Raya narrowed her eyes. "He's bluffing. If he could've freed himself from the summoning, he would have left already. He's just trying to scare us."

"Why did he even show up in the first place? We summoned Andy, not this demon."

Raya shrugged. "This isn't exactly precision stuff."

"Excuse me? I'm sorry, am I interrupting?" He waggled the flutes at them.

Erin glared at him. "Shut up."

The demon's eyebrows shot up and his wings dropped a few inches.

"I'm not a witch. I'm Erin. I want my friend Andy back, and you're going to promise to help find him, or she's going to blast you. Are we clear?"

His bluster faded. "All right, you don't have to be such a pill about it."

She didn't dare take her eyes off him. "Raya? What do we do now? Can you make him sign some kind of binding something-or-other?"

Phoenix pressed the back of his hand against his forehead and closed his eyes. "For the love of all that's unholy. A binding something-or-other? Really? Is that what I've come to?"

"Again—demon, shut up," said Raya. She addressed Erin. "He has to be bound in some way. Otherwise he'll just take off at the first chance."

"You wound me," said Phoenix, pressing the champagne bottle over his chest, where his heart would be, if he had one.

Blaze barked joyfully and surged into the kitchen.

"Blaze, no!" said Raya.

Erin realized as she lunged for the dog that the banging sound hadn't been from the spell—it had been the sound of Blaze ramming the dog gate.

The dog barrelled past her and slid into the salt ring like a baseball player sliding home.

A snapping sound cracked across the kitchen, accompanied by a shower of sparks.

The demon in the circle grinned triumphantly.

"He's escaping!" said Erin.

The dog barked wildly as the candles extinguished themselves, leaving the kitchen in darkness.

14

Erin made her way to the light switch and flipped on the lights. The demon lay sprawled in the middle of the kitchen floor with Blaze draped across his chest.

Raya stood over them with her wand raised. "Hold still, demon!"

"Get this beast off me, witch!"

Blaze licked his face with a large and very slobbery tongue.

"Oh, gross!" he said, using his fingers to wipe away the drool. "I give up. I'll do whatever you want. Just get this thing off me."

"Good dog," said Raya, patting the hefty dog's back.

Erin picked her way through the detritus of salt, rose petals, and other assorted ingredients to stand beside Raya. "What happened?"

"He tried to escape, and Blaze stopped him." She tugged at Blaze's collar. "Come on, old girl."

The dog clambered up and skidded on the mess on the floor, none the worse for wear.

The demon maneuvered himself to sit up against the oven. "That's not playing fair, you know. Siccing hellhounds on innocent demons."

"No one asked your opinion," said Raya.

Erin eyed the demon. "So who is this guy, anyway?"

"Are you going to talk about me like I'm not here? Rude."

"Fine. I'm Raya, this is Erin, and you are?"

The demon tugged at his cuffs and ran his hands over his hair before replying. "Phoenix. Great Marquis of Hell. Poet, scholar, life of the party, and demon-about-town." He stood up, stretched his red wings to their full length, then snapped them away. "So you want to find Andy, do you?"

Erin felt hope bloom within her. "You know him, then?"

Phoenix waved his hand through the air dismissively. "Sure I do. Andromalius. Chap with the red bow tie and too much time on his hands. How did you manage to lose him in the first place?"

"She blasted him."

Phoenix laughed. "Brilliant."

"Can't you just call him up?"

"Call him up? It doesn't work that way, as any witch worth her salt could have told you." He eyed Raya meaningfully.

The tips of Raya's ears turned pink and she opened her mouth to speak.

Erin cut her off. "Why don't we all adjourn to the living room and figure this out? The sooner we get started, the sooner we'll all be done."

"Anyone seen my champagne?" Phoenix clapped his hands together and looked around the kitchen. He spotted the bottle where it had rolled under the cabinets. He retrieved the bottle and set about opening it.

"Are you...drinking? Now?" said Erin.

"Is there a better time for drinking?" He popped the cork and put the bottle to his lips, then drank deeply and wiped his mouth on his sleeve. "I'm sorry. Did you want some?" He held the bottle out to Erin.

Erin shook her head.

"What about you, Witchiepoo?" He offered it to Raya.

"Go to Hell," said Raya.

"Oh, say it like you mean it, darling," said Phoenix, and knocked back another swig.

Erin shooed the demon and the witch out of the kitchen before Raya had a chance to take a swing at Phoenix.

Blaze followed them, her large paws thumping on the floor.

Phoenix sprawled on the couch, wine bottle in hand.

Erin sat on the other end of the couch, primly avoiding his outstretched legs. "Can he actually get drunk?"

Raya sat cross-legged on a rag rug. "If he wants to."

"You bet I want to," said Phoenix.

Erin stood up and paced the room. As she passed Phoenix, she grabbed the wine bottle. "That's enough of that. Sit up."

Phoenix cast her an aggrieved look. "Oh, come on, give a chap a break."

"Do what she says," said Raya.

"Outnumbered," said Phoenix. He followed it with a deep sigh and sat up. "Conjured, kidnapped, and outnumbered, and they won't even let me have a little bubbly to take the edge off."

"Also, shut up," said Raya.

Phoenix lapsed into a silence that projected maximum self-pity.

"What's the best way to do this?" asked Erin. "How do we find Andromalius?"

Phoenix laced his fingers behind his head and leaned back. "What your trigger-happy witch friend accomplished was the equivalent of knocking someone out. He's not in Hell, or somewhere else on planet Earth. He's gone right out of conscious existence."

"How do I wake him up, then?"

"I haven't the faintest idea. He'll show up. Or he won't. Can I have the bottle back, now?"

"No," said Erin. "So this was a waste of time?"

"You got to meet me, didn't you? How many mortals can say they've met Phoenix, a Great Marquis of Hell?"

Raya stood up and joined Phoenix on the couch. "You're right." She snaked an arm around the demon, who looked distinctly uncomfortable. "We are so lucky to have met you."

"Quite right," said Phoenix, fidgeting under her touch.

"In fact, now that I know you can't help with finding her demon, I'm beginning to think of all the ways you could make up for your unfulfilled promise to help," said Raya, squeezing his shoulder.

"Steady on," said Phoenix.

"My lawn could use some work," said Raya. "And, come to think of it, the gutters haven't been cleaned in ages."

"Lawn work?" said Phoenix, nearly choking on the words. "You can't be serious. You don't summon a Marquis of Hell to do your lawn work."

"If he's not useful for anything else…" Raya examined her nails.

"Hang on a second," said Phoenix. "Let's not be hasty. I'm sure I can help you call Andy up."

"You can?" said Erin. "I thought you said there wasn't anything you could do."

"He just needed some motivation. Isn't that right, pet?" Raya gave Phoenix a little shake.

Phoenix swallowed. "Right," he croaked.

Erin looked back and forth between the witch and the demon. Surely they could help.

At least, they couldn't possibly make anything worse.

15

Erin sat in her car in the church parking lot and wondered why she'd bothered to come. It might keep her mother off her back temporarily, but was it worth it?

Why was she here?

Going to church just to annoy Mark didn't feel as satisfying as it had before.

She watched the parishioners trickle in from the parking lot. It was almost time for the service to begin. Her mother was most likely already inside the church. Erin hadn't even spotted Mark and Genevieve, and in the place of morbid curiosity, she found a tentative but growing feeling of indifference.

Erin dragged her purse out of the front passenger seat and into her lap. She removed the keys from the ignition, and put them in her purse. She put her hand on the door handle.

She didn't open it.

Instead, she sat, frozen with indecision, until a memory of

Mark's pantsing flitted across her mind. She cackled aloud and her hand dropped from the door handle. Nothing could ever top that. She could go to church services every Sunday for the rest of her life, but they would always be a disappointment compared to the day that Andy showed up.

Erin pulled her keys out of her purse and tossed the purse back onto the passenger's seat. She started the car and drove out of the parking lot, headed for the highway onramp just a few blocks away.

She drove through many miles of pine forest. Eventually, the forest thinned to reveal thick grass and tangled shrub bordering the edges of a swamp-like river that glimmered beneath the highway bridge.

Erin pulled off the next exit and followed the two lane road along the river's edge all the way to a sleepy downtown neighborhood.

An assortment of colorful whirligigs and flags fluttered in the yard of an old Victorian house facing a quiet side street. The sign on the veranda read "The Dragon's Cave: Olde Worlde Curiosities and Magical Supplies."

This was certainly a different way to spend a Sunday.

Erin pulled into the driveway underneath an old oak tree draped with Spanish moss.

She'd passed the quaint magic shop dozens of times over the years, when in the neighborhood for an ordinary outing of shopping and dining, but never once set foot in the store. The gravel crunched under her feet as she approached the house.

The stained glass in the heavy wooden door was impossible to see through. Erin pushed the door open carefully, setting a tangle of bells to ringing as she stepped over the threshold.

Mismatched bookshelves and shabby glass cases lined the walls. Woven baskets mixed higgledy-piggledy with plastic buckets on the shelves, each filled with crystals, incense cones, or some other magical accoutrement.

Erin idly picked up a piece of rose quartz and weighed it in her hand.

"That's for love," a voice piped up.

Erin turned in the direction of the voice.

A young girl sat behind a cash register. Her colorful dress draped the stool she perched on with yards of overflowing fabric. She tilted her head and focused her large hazel eyes on Erin. "Are you looking for a love charm?" Her childlike features contrasted with the vintage hippie aesthetic of her clothing, making her look simultaneously young and old.

"Um. No," said Erin, placing the rose quartz back in its basket. "Is your mommy around?"

"She's upstairs. She'll be back in a few minutes. Can I help you?" The girl slid off the stool, eager to assist.

"I think I'll just look around," said Erin.

"Sure. Okay." The girl quieted, but stared unselfconsciously at Erin, following her every movement.

When Erin picked up a book, the girl approached. "Are you studying hedge magic? That's a good one. I like the forest stuff. It's really helpful. Do you like forests?"

Erin put the book down. "I don't know."

"Then why did you pick that one up? Silly. You need help."

"Probably," said Erin.

The girl nodded, sending her fine brown hair swishing back and forth. "How about we start with a nice wand?"

Erin hesitated. Raya had done a lot with her wand, maybe even too much. The idea of a wand intimidated her.

"No wand?"

"Maybe not yet. Maybe when I know what I'm doing," said Erin.

The girl shrugged. "Okay. How about cards?"

"Cards?"

"Fortune-telling cards. You know. Tarot?"

"I don't know…"

"I know! I'll read them for you. Then you can see if you like them and you can buy some of your own. Come!" The girl skipped to the counter and pulled out a velvet bag.

"You sure your mommy won't mind?"

The girl beamed. "Mommy says I'm the best. She won't mind at all."

"Try before you buy," said Erin.

"Exactly!" The girl's musical laugh echoed in the otherwise empty shop. "Now, when I read the cards for someone, they have to focus on what it is they want. You do know what you want, right?"

"I'm not sure, actually."

The girl tsk-tsked. "The first step in getting what you want is knowing what you want. I thought everybody knew that." She eyed Erin skeptically.

"I guess—I thought I knew what I wanted, but I didn't."

"You really do need help, don't you?"

Erin chuckled. "I guess I do."

"Close your eyes, then."

"What?"

"Close them!" The girl fluttered her hands at Erin.

Erin obeyed.

"Picture yourself standing in a forest. Grass underneath your feet. Trees soaring into the air around you. The sun breaking through the leaves to warm you. Can you see it?"

Erin nodded.

"Now look into the distance. See the hills on the horizon?"

"Yes. I see them."

"There's a road before you. It runs from where you stand all the way to the hills. Can you see the road?"

A sliver of anxiety slid through Erin. "I don't know where it goes."

"Don't be afraid," said the girl. "Just look down the road. Follow it with your eyes as far as you can see."

Erin breathed deeply and placed her hands on the edge of the counter for balance. In her mind's eye, she looked down the road, farther and farther.

"What do you see where the road disappears over the hill?"

"I see—" All of a sudden, she saw the silhouette of wings rising over the hill, as if something were coming over the hill from the other side to meet her. "I see someone."

"Do you know this person?"

"I do."

"Okay, then. You can open your eyes now."

Erin looked at the strange girl.

"That's the goal you're headed toward right now. Reach that, and the next time you visualize the road, you might see something different."

"You're very wise," said Erin.

"Mommy says I'm an old soul." The girl opened the velvet bag, removed a large deck of cards, and shuffled them. "Now that you have a goal, I can read the cards for you." She turned over the first card. "The first card is the past. You got the Tower, which means that you had a big change. Probably an unexpected one. Everything you thought was strong and steady fell down around your ears, basically."

"I'll say," said Erin.

The girl laid down a second card. "This is the present. You got the Star. Magic is flowing around you. There is great potential if you follow the voice within."

"That sounds good," said Erin, feeling cautiously optimistic.

"I like the Star. It's a good one." The girl drew a third card and turned it over, revealing a wheel surrounded by creatures. "The future. The Wheel of Fortune."

"Is that good?"

"It is what it is. The Wheel means change. Where you were is different than where you will end up. It also symbolizes karma." The girl's gaze met Erin's. "What goes around, comes around."

The Tower, the Star, and the Wheel of Fortune settled in Erin's mind like gems in a setting. "Thank you. I think you helped a lot."

"Do you want to get your own set?" The girl's hazel eyes blazed with hope.

"I think I will. Give me a set like yours. And—you know what? You got anything for good luck? Good dreams? Anything like that?"

"Have I? Have I ever!" The girl bounded out from behind the counter. She grabbed a handful of crystals and stacked several books in the crook of her arm. "These are just what you need."

"Great. Anything else you would recommend?" she asked, throwing herself fully on the judgment of the precocious child.

The girl looked her up and down. "Let me see. I know you said you didn't want a wand, but how about a necklace?" She ducked behind the counter and retrieved a clear crystal dangling from a silver chain. "This one is good for everything."

"I'll take it."

The girl piled Erin's purchases on the counter and pecked the cash register with two fingers to add up the total.

Erin handed over cash and received her change.

The girl hummed a tune as she wrapped the more delicate items in tissue paper and slipped each one into the bag.

The sound of footsteps on old wooden stairs echoed through the room.

"Mommy!" called the girl. "Look at all the things this nice lady bought."

The girl's mother emerged into the front room. "Oh, my. Have you been a good salesperson?" Unlike her daughter, the older woman was dressed in casual slacks and a blouse that wouldn't have been out of place in a more conventional workplace.

"She got the quartz crystal necklace." The girl picked it up. It was the only item remaining that hadn't been packed into the bag. "You want to wear it to go?"

Erin looked back and forth between the girl and the shop owner. "Sure. Yes." She reached across the counter and took the necklace from the girl's fingers. Triggering the clasp open, she drew the necklace around the back of her neck and re-clasped it, letting the sparkling crystal fall into place on her chest. She touched it self-consciously. "Thank you."

"I hope it's everything she promised you," said the woman, handing over Erin's bag.

"I have no doubt of that," said Erin.

"Come back and tell me how it worked!" the girl called as Erin pushed open the door of the shop.

"I will!" Erin turned and waved goodbye before the heavy door swung closed with a final rattle of bells.

16

When the phone rang, Erin dove across the bed to retrieve it, narrowly missing Nancy Drew, who blinked at her myopically before trotting out of the way. Erin picked up the phone and mashed the button to answer.

Raya's voice crackled through the handset. "Hey. What are you doing?"

"Nothing. Just hanging out and reading."

"Reading what?"

Erin glanced at the pile of books from the magic shop and made a quick decision to keep that field trip to herself for the moment. "Nothing much."

"Glad to hear it. Well, put your pants on and get ready to go. I'll pick you up."

Erin sat up. "Where are we going?"

"I'll tell you when I get there. See you in fifteen." Raya hung up.

Erin stared at the phone before dropping it back in its cradle. "Looks like I'm going out," she said to Nancy. "Think you can keep an eye on things while I'm gone?"

Nancy Drew cocked her head.

"I thought so. Come on, girl." She let Nancy out into the backyard before returning to the bedroom to freshen up. She removed the books from the bed and stacked them on one of the bedside tables next to her small collection of crystals.

It would have been nice to know where they were going, but Raya seemed to enjoy being mysterious. In any case, the weather hardly varied during the summer—scorching hot, of course—making it easy to choose an outfit. Erin pulled on a tank top and shorts, then added a pair of flat sandals and a wide-brimmed hat. The necklace still hung around her neck—she hadn't taken it off except to shower—and as she checked her appearance in the mirror, the crystal sparkled as it shifted from side to side.

She brought Nancy Drew inside and filled the doggie bowls with food and fresh water. "See you later, Nancy," she said, ruffling the dog's soft ears.

At the sound of Raya's car pulling into the driveway, Nancy put on her sunglasses and left the house, locking the front door. She walked down the driveway to Raya's truck.

The passenger window rolled down. "Get in," said Raya.

Erin slid into the passenger seat. "So what's the big mystery? And where's Phoenix?"

"Not like he'd fit." Raya gestured to the truck cab. "Plus, we were getting on each other's nerves. So I sent him to follow Mark around."

"You what?" Erin whipped off her sunglasses and stared at Raya.

Raya shrugged. "He seemed to like the idea."

"Of course he would. He's a demon. But how's that going to help?"

"You're not getting squeamish, are you? Miss I-Summon-Demons-for-Revenge?" Raya pressed the accelerator and the truck shot ahead. "Come on, you have to be just a little curious about what your ex is up to. The more you know, the better you can plan your revenge. Isn't that why you wanted Andy back?" Raya cast Erin a sidelong look before returning her gaze to the road.

Erin's mouth opened and shut while she considered her answer.

Raya didn't wait for one. "Anyway, since your ex was the key to Andy showing up, he might be the key to getting Andy back."

"So where are we going?"

"Phoenix said Mark and Genevieve spent the whole day hanging around the big fancy hotel next to Destiny Park."

"Le Nouveau Palmier?"

Raya nodded. "That's the one. Phoenix said they didn't stay overnight. They just walked around a lot. Like they were planning something. Does he have a lot of money?" asked Raya.

"Who, Mark? More than me. He has a higher-paying job by far. And a better house. That's why I was going to sell mine after I married Mark. But the market wasn't great, so it just sat there."

"Thank God," said Raya, pulling onto the highway.

"Thank God," echoed Erin, wondering where God fit in, exactly, in the plans of a witch, two demons, and a divorcée with an elderly dog. She stared out the window as they zipped past pine forests under the blazing midday sun.

"Besides, whether we get anything out of this or not, it's a good excuse to get out of the house. Sit by the pool, you know?

Have a few margaritas." Raya performed an impromptu dance by wiggling in her seat.

"So is this really about revenge, or getting Andy back, or getting out of the house?"

Raya shrugged philosophically. "Who says you can't have it all?"

They drove in silence for a while, until they were well past the exit Erin had taken to the magic shop the other day.

At the palm tree-lined entrance to Le Nouveau Palmier, Erin wondered how they would pass the security gate, considering that they had no hotel reservation and no real reason to be there.

Raya rolled down her window to speak to the security guard. "We're going to lunch," she said, in a very un-Raya-like tone of mild amiability.

Erin turned her head away so the guard wouldn't see her suppress a laugh.

"Of course," said the guard. He tipped his navy blue hat. "You ladies have a marvelous day."

"Why, thank you," Raya said, with pure sugar in her voice.

"Thanks," said Erin, giving a little wave to the guard as they pulled away. "What was that? 'Oh, why thank you kindly, kind sir!'" she said, mimicking Raya's delivery.

"It worked, didn't it?"

"I guess some magic you don't need a wand for," said Erin.

"Now you're catching on," said Raya. "We'll make a witch of you yet."

Erin touched the crystal on her necklace.

After parking the truck, they approached the front of the hotel on a smooth sidewalk lined with stately palm trees and curved flower beds. Ornate twists of green-painted wrought iron criss-crossed over the porte cochere like graceful metallic vines. Flowers and trees glittered in fine mosaics across the facade. The stonework curved around windows and balconies all the way to the multicolored gingerbread roof tiles.

They crossed a threshold depicting a stylized mosaic palm tree encircled in two gold rings.

"This way," said Raya, leading Erin through the glass-covered arcade enclosing the lobby.

It was tempting to stop and gawk, but Erin kept walking. "You've been here before," she said.

"You bet I have. I love Art Deco stuff," said Raya.

"This is amazing," said Erin, stumbling slightly as she tried to look all around while keeping up with Raya.

"Wait till you see the pool."

"Aren't we supposed to be trying to figure out what Mark and Genevieve were doing?"

Raya waved away Erin's objection like she was swatting a fly. "Sure, sure. After some drinks."

They found a pair of vacant lounge chairs a short distance from the pool and settled into them.

Raya hailed the pool attendant. "Two Singapore Slings, please." She turned to Erin. "My treat."

The attendant, a young man garbed in a crisp white shirt and shorts, jogged off immediately to fulfill the order.

The sunlight sparkled on the surface of the pool and glinted its way through an assortment of playful fountains and tiny waterfalls ringing the pool area.

When Erin received her drink, she held it up to the light and admired it. "Isn't that pretty?"

Raya sipped and smacked her lips. "Tastes as good as it looks."

Erin tasted the drink carefully, knowing that even a little alcohol went straight to her head. "Mm. You're not wrong." She let her head rest against the pool chair while she held the cold cocktail glass in her hands. "Can I ask you something?"

Raya tipped her glass back. "Go for it."

Erin glanced around to check if anyone was within earshot before speaking. "How did you become a witch?"

Raya set her glass down and smiled. "That's quite a question."

"Well?"

"Why do you ask?"

"Why do I ask? Because, one, I've never met one before—"

"That you know of," said Raya.

"That I know of," agreed Erin. "And, two, it must be an interesting story. I mean, I grew up going to a regular old church. Did you grow up going to—I don't know—witch school?"

Raya laughed. "Witch school! Hardly. My family wasn't particularly religious in any direction. I started reading books about magic when I was in high school—you know, as teenage girls will do—and I liked the whole idea of having some kind of power."

"I didn't think anything like that was even real," said Erin.

"You went to church, though. You believed in all kinds of things," Raya said.

"Sure, but that's more taking things on faith than seeing an actual demonstration. Meeting Andy—and then seeing you send him away—was pretty impressive."

"Eh." Raya drank from her glass and looked thoughtful. "You prayed in your way, I prayed in mine. We probably both had times where we felt our prayers were answered."

"I guess you're right," said Erin. "Still, that was pretty dramatic. I've never banished a demon before."

"You never tried to," said Raya.

"Good point." Erin's gaze drifted over the pool. "It's one thing to believe in something. It's another thing altogether to see it for real before your eyes. When I saw Andy for the first time, he spread his wings right there in the kitchen—to prove what he was, you know? And I was shocked, but at the same time, I thought, 'Of course.' Like it was a confirmation of what I'd believed all along."

"Exactly."

"If demons are real, and witches are real, what else is out there? Angels? Where is God in all this? What about other religions?"

"That's above my pay grade," said Raya.

Erin shifted onto her side and faced Raya. "Don't you think about it? What's out there? Where did it come from?"

"Who knows?"

"Has Phoenix said anything about it?"

Raya scoffed. "Phoenix? He's too busy thinking the universe revolves around him to put any serious thought into the actual nature of the universe."

"I just want to know if all this is a product of human belief, or some great unknown force." Erin tipped her glass back and drank the last of her Singapore Sling. Sure enough, it had gone straight to her head. She stared into the empty glass. "My beliefs seem to have manifested as a demon in a red suit and bow tie with a really good massage technique."

"Well, mine manifested as an English-accented demon with an attitude and a drinking problem. Go figure. Speak of the devil…"

Erin sat up straight. "What?"

"Isn't that Phoenix?" said Raya.

17

Phoenix sauntered into the pool area like he owned it. He carried an old fashioned glass brimming with amber liquid over ice and mint leaves. As he walked, he sipped from the rim as if to prevent spilling the drink on his white linen suit.

"Hello, Witchiepoo," he said, addressing Raya.

"What the hell are you doing here?" she replied.

"Thought you might like to know"—he paused for a leisurely sip—"the quarry decided to make a return trip."

"What do you mean?" said Erin.

"He means they came back," said Raya.

Phoenix raised his eyebrows in an insinuating manner.

"Who came back?" Erin asked. His meaning cut through the alcohol-induced fog in her brain all in one flash. "Oh, my God! Mark and Genevieve are here?" She looked all around.

"Calm down," said Raya. "Don't make yourself conspicuous."

"But what if they think I followed them here?"

"You kind of did," said Phoenix.

"Oh, my God," repeated Erin. She dropped her head into her hands. "We have to go."

"No way," said Raya. "Now we can see for ourselves what they're up to. Aren't you curious?"

The situation was spiraling rapidly out of control. "Yes, but not enough to humiliate myself by following my ex-husband and ex-best friend around a hotel."

"Come on. Live a little," said Raya. She stood up, then bent over and tugged Erin's hat lower. "See, they'll never recognize you."

Erin crossed her arms over her chest. "Yes, they will."

"Just stay behind us," said Raya.

"Us?" said Phoenix.

"Yes, us, you idiot demon—unless you'd rather head back and work on the lawn?"

"When you put it like that, Your Majesty, how can I resist?" Phoenix bowed mockingly.

"This is a bad idea," said Erin.

"Of course it is," said Phoenix. "But we are all in thrall to Her Royal Witchiness."

"Shut up, Phoenix," said Raya.

"Oh, she used my name! Will wonders never cease!" said Phoenix.

Erin dragged her legs off the lounge chair and slowly stood, her head spinning from the drink. "Fine."

Raya and Phoenix walked side by side, with Erin trailing just behind. They exited the pool area and followed the meandering garden paths back to the lobby, where Erin hung back behind a sculpted stone column while Raya and Phoenix scanned the lobby crowd.

"There they are," said Raya.

Genevieve leaned on Mark, her arm entwined through his as they walked through the lobby. They did not stop to admire the decorations but cut straight through to a smaller arcade on the far side of the lobby.

Raya and Phoenix took off in their wake, maintaining a careful distance from Mark and Genevieve.

Erin tugged at her hat repeatedly, trying to pull it even lower as she trailed Raya and Phoenix.

When Mark and Genevieve paused to admire an especially elaborate flower arrangement, Raya, Phoenix, and Erin quickly pivoted to study the glass storefront display of one of the hotel's gift shops.

When the couple moved on, the trio continued following them.

"The crowd is thinning out," Erin whispered. "We'll be too obvious."

Raya turned her head and whispered back, "There aren't too many places they can go from here. We'll turn back in a minute if we don't see anything."

Erin's caution proved premature when Mark and Genevieve abruptly turned off into a smaller hallway off the arcade, then disappeared.

Raya peeked around the corner. "They're gone."

"Where did they go?" Erin peeked over Raya's shoulder. Several signs hung from the hallway ceiling, indicating different rooms. She read them aloud one by one. "Salon de Coiffure. Le Spa. Le Organisateur de Mariage."

"Oh, my," said Phoenix. He chuckled and shook the remaining ice in his glass, which clinked gently, the sounds echoing in the marble-tiled hallway.

"Organisateur…" said Erin, uncertainly.

"Organizer," said Phoenix, appearing to enjoy himself hugely.

"The organizer of…marriage?"

"Give the lady a prize," said Phoenix, raising his glass to her.

"They're getting married? Already?" The Singapore Sling in her stomach threatened to reappear.

"Easy, there," said Raya, steering her away from the little hallway. "Why don't we go sit down?"

"Sit down? I can't sit down! What if they come back out and see me?"

"Fine," said Raya. "Back to the truck. Demon, we'll see you later."

"What, I can't catch a ride in your truck bed? My heart breaks."

"Get lost," said Raya, who had looped her arm through Erin's and was practically frog-marching her out of the hotel.

Phoenix smirked. "I needed a refill anyway. Goodbye, Your Witchiness." He nodded to Erin and strolled away, in the direction of the bar.

"I can walk," said Erin. "You don't need to drag me."

Raya loosened her hold. "I didn't want you to keel over from shock while we were still inside."

"I'm not keeling over," said Erin. "I'm just a little surprised, that's all."

"Sure. Surprised. That's why you looked like you were going to explode on the spot."

They reached Raya's truck and got in.

In the confined space, Erin could hear her own breath, which came faster than normal—and not just from fleeing the hotel. "I'm not upset about them," she said. "I'm upset at myself. Why am I following them around? Why did I run away? They can get married or fly to the moon, for all I care."

Raya turned the key in the ignition, sending ice-cold air blasting into the cab. "Well, that's great! You're more over Mark than you thought."

"I don't care what he does. Or what they do."

"And now you know that." Raya threw the truck into reverse and backed out of the parking spot.

"I guess I kind of knew it all along—stop!"

Raya hit the brakes, the sudden stop slamming both women against their seatbelts. "What is it?"

"I don't want to leave."

"You don't?"

"Let's go back to the pool."

"Really?" Raya peered at Erin.

"Really. They got a gift shop here?"

"Sure…" Raya eased the truck back into the parking space.

"Great. You want to go swimming?"

"Um—"

Erin unbuckled her seatbelt. "I'm going swimming." She opened the door and slid out of the truck.

Raya hastily turned off the truck and followed her into the hotel.

Erin marched into the gift shop and found a rack of overpriced bathing suits. She rifled through the rack until she found her size. "How about you?"

"This one." Raya took a suit for herself.

"My treat," said Erin, holding out her hand for Raya's choice of bathing suit.

Raya handed it to her.

Erin purchased the suits and strode to the pool area. She handed the other suit to Raya.

They used the changing room to slip into their newly purchased suits, then emerged with bare feet onto the warm concrete pool deck.

"Back so soon, ladies?" Phoenix's voice carried from his perch on a nearby lounge chair.

Erin dropped her things on the chair and closed her eyes, tilting her face upward to the rays of the sun.

She opened her eyes and smiled. With quick steps, she closed the distance to the edge of the pool and cannonballed into the deep end.

18

Erin ignored the flashing light on the answering machine and followed Nancy Drew out into the backyard. She settled in one of the two chairs on the back porch to watch Nancy cavort in the sparse grass under the gathering storm clouds.

Her gaze swept the sandy backyard as she considered planting flowers. A rose bush over here, perhaps, and a container garden of succulents over there. Right now there wasn't a lot of money for anything extra—especially after the swimsuits—but it didn't hurt to dream.

She toyed with the crystal on her necklace and watched tiny flickers of concentrated sunlight dance. Of course she was stalling rather than doing what she needed to do—namely, listen to her voicemail message, which was most likely from her mother, who would demand to know why she hadn't been at church on Sunday. Explaining that she'd been at a magic shop buying a bag full of magic paraphernalia probably wouldn't go over well.

Erin let her mind drift back to the magic shop.

The sound of Nancy barking at her feet brought her back to the present. "Okay, girl," she said. "I'm coming." She stood up and went inside with the dog at her heels.

In the kitchen, the answering machine continued to blink its red light on and off. She pressed the button and waited to hear her mother's voice.

"Erin, it's me," said the recording.

It wasn't her mother.

It was Genevieve.

"I was hoping we could talk. Please call me."

Erin froze, gripping the edge of the kitchen counter. After all this time, she wanted to talk? About what? Erin's hand darted out and hit the button again.

"Erin, it's me. I was hoping we could talk. Please call me," said the machine, with Genevieve's voice.

Nancy Drew trotted over at the familiar sound and looked up at Erin expectantly.

"She's not here, baby," said Erin.

Nancy Drew's ears perked up.

"Poor old dog. You can't understand any of this, can you?" Erin kneeled and gave Nancy a dog biscuit and a gentle scratch on the head. "Everyone is a friend to you. But not to me."

Erin debated her options.

Raya would have told her to raise both middle fingers to the answering machine and delete the message. Andy would have suggested letting the air out of all four of the tires on Genevieve's car. Her mother, on the other hand, would probably advise Erin to take the high road—while Joyce secretly did the dirty work of spreading juicy gossip about Genevieve.

Her emotions couldn't possibly be any more confused. Outside, rain began to pour, making a cacophonous yet soothing sound on the roof.

She picked up the phone, tossed it from hand to hand, then dropped it back in the cradle and walked to the bedroom, where she picked up the pile of tarot cards and the matching booklet from her bedside table.

Cards in hand, she sat down on the living room floor.

Nancy Drew sat down next to her, pressing her furry body against Erin's leg.

Erin spread out the cards on the coffee table, searching for the ones the girl had drawn at the magic shop. She picked up the Tower, the Star, and the Wheel of Fortune and laid them in a row. Erin touched the Tower card with one finger, then turned to its page in the booklet and read aloud. "Destruction. Change. Liberation." Inspired, she jumped up and ran to the kitchen, where she retrieved the wedding album from under the counter. She brought the album to the living room and placed it on the coffee table with the Tower card on top of it.

"The Star," she murmured, turning her attention to the second card. She found herself touching the crystal hanging from her necklace. She found the relevant page in the booklet and read aloud. "Spiritual inspiration. Renewal. Hope." Erin considered for a moment, then unclasped the necklace and laid it on the card.

"The Wheel of Fortune." This one was more complicated. Erin considered the card as she slowly rotated it on the surface of the table. When it completed a full revolution, she picked it up and held it in her cupped hands. She closed her eyes and sought inspiration within. A long-ago lesson returned to mind, and she spoke it aloud over the card. "When men are cast down, then thou shalt say, There is lifting up; and he shall save the humble person."

Erin chuckled. God must have a sense of humor. Why else would she recall an obscure Bible verse from the Book of Job in the middle of seeking spiritual inspiration for conjuring a friendly demon? Where she had expected to find conflict between two different systems of belief, she found only a sense of completion, like a key fitting into a lock—possibly sacrilegious, but satisfying all the same.

She looked around the room. Her gaze landed on one of the markers Andy had so enthusiastically used to plot revenge. She picked it up and held it in both hands. What he had written was proof he had been here. Erin laid the marker on the Wheel of Fortune card, patting it for good measure, then gathered the rest of the deck and shuffled the cards.

"If a kid can do it, so can I," she said. "Right, Nancy?"

Nancy's tail thumped the floor.

"One card," she said. "For guidance." Erin tapped the top of the deck and drew one card, laying it face up on the coffee table, separate from the Tower, the Star, and the Wheel of Fortune. "The Nine of Wands. What's that?" She flipped through the booklet and scanned the page for the Nine of Wands, picking out the salient words. "Battle fatigue. Standing up for yourself. Persistence. Close to success. How about that, Nancy?"

Nancy scratched herself with a back paw.

Erin returned to the bedroom and collected the assortment of crystals from her bedside table. She piled all of them on the Nine of Wands, then dusted her hands. "I'm all in."

Nancy stood up and poked her head over the coffee table, sniffing hopefully at the stones.

Erin stared at the array on the coffee table. She touched each card one more time—the Tower, the Star, the Wheel of Fortune, and the Nine of Wands—before walking into the kitchen.

She took a deep breath and picked up the phone. She dialed a familiar number.

"Genevieve? It's me, Erin."

19

The coffee shop had been Erin and Genevieve's favorite meeting place. Now a painful reminder of betrayal and loss, Erin had avoided the cozy cafe ever since she found out Mark was cheating on her. She'd visited it only in dreams—and even then, not by choice. Genevieve's suggestion that they meet in person to talk brought to the surface a flood of emotions Erin would have preferred to stay buried.

When Erin ducked out of the rain and into the coffee shop, she almost expected to see Andy waiting for her, wearing his red suit, with his wings unfurled. Erin smiled at the memory of when he accompanied her into her own dreams. What a shock it would be to the coffee shop patrons to look up and see a demon over their rainy afternoon coffees.

If only he were really there.

Erin sighed and ordered a coffee from the counter. After the barista handed her the mug, Erin looked around for her former best friend.

Genevieve sat at a corner cafe table. She was without coffee of any kind, which was unusual. She wore little make-up, and her hair hung at half-mast in a ponytail that almost looked messy, and not in an artfully disarrayed fashion, either.

Erin slid into a chair facing Genevieve. "Hi."

"Hi," said Genevieve.

The awkward exchange made Erin's skin prickle with goosebumps. She waited for Genevieve to continue.

"Thank you for coming," said Genevieve. Without a coffee cup to cradle, her hands clasped and unclasped nervously on the table.

"No coffee today?" asked Erin.

Genevieve shook her head. "I'm off it."

Erin had nothing to add to that.

"Erin, I know we haven't talked since…well, you know how long we haven't talked. But I have some things I want to say to you. I hope you'll give me a chance to say them."

Erin sat back and gave Genevieve her full attention. "Go ahead."

"First, I want you to know that I'm sorry. I'm so sorry I hurt you. I'm not asking for your forgiveness. You don't owe me that. But I want you to know I'm sorry."

Erin nodded but said nothing.

"Second—I know it doesn't matter—but things haven't turned out quite like I pictured. I don't know if you'll find any satisfaction in that, but there it is."

"If you were going to ruin our friendship over a man, I guess you would hope it turned out well," said Erin, with a tone almost as bitter as the coffee in her cup.

"I deserved that," said Genevieve, holding her hands up in a stop-don't-shoot gesture. "Third—there's something else."

"Yes?"

"I'm pregnant."

Erin nearly spat out a mouthful of coffee. "You're what?"

"I'm pregnant, Erin."

Erin felt like she'd dodged a bullet. After what she'd learned about Mark's character, she was relieved he would never be the father of her children. Erin took a sip of her coffee to cover a small smile as she recalled her mother pointing out Genevieve getting "chubby." Joyce would never stop crowing about her observation once she found out this news. "Why are you telling me?"

"I don't know. It seemed right, somehow. Even if I did everything else wrong, I could at least be the first to tell you. I didn't want you to hear it secondhand." Genevieve rested her hand on her belly. "And that brings me to the last thing."

"Which is?"

"Which is that Mark and I are going to get married."

"I know."

"You know?"

"Word gets around," said Erin.

Genevieve gave her a long, speculative look. "Okay. Here's the thing. I know Mark tried to get you to stop coming to church. But I don't agree with him—it would be wrong to chase you away just to save us discomfort, when you didn't even do anything wrong. And maybe you don't have any interest in coming to church anymore—that's your business—but I don't want to be the one to drive you off." She took a deep breath. "On top of that, our wedding is going to be at the church, and you are invited to come."

"Wow," said Erin, setting down her mug. "I'm invited to come to the wedding of my cheating ex-husband and my ex-best friend. This is one for the books."

Genevieve winced. "Don't take it that way." She looked down at the table. "I'm probably not saying any of this right."

Erin caught herself about to make a comforting remark, the kind you make in casual conversation to smooth over the rough patches. The impulse took her by surprise.

"I'm not saying I made good choices. But I'm going to have to live with them. And I don't want my choices to affect you any more than they already have." She looked up at Erin. "You're destined for something better."

Genevieve's words sent a ripple of pity through Erin. Who would want to be married to Mark, anyway?

The realization shattered the last remaining chains she hadn't even known she'd been wearing.

"Well, this has been most interesting," said Erin. "Thank you for what you said. I am glad I heard it from you. And thank you for the invitation. Don't think this means I forgive you—I don't—but I think you might be right about one thing. I am destined for better things." She stood up. "In fact, I need to see a girl about a crystal. Goodbye, Genevieve." She left Genevieve alone at the table and strode to the exit, feeling the swing of her hips as she walked with purpose and momentum out the door.

The storm clouds above swirled and broke, revealing patches of blue sky.

The drive to the magic shop seemed quicker than the first time. Erin parked under the old oak tree and jogged up the steps to the door. She pushed it open and peered inside. "Hello?"

Thumping footsteps echoed through the wooden floor. The card-reading girl, now wearing a different bohemian dress, bounded into the front room. "You're back! Did you like all the stuff?"

"Hi, there. Yes, I'm back. And I did like it. So much so that I've come back for more."

"Hot dog," said the girl. "You want a wand now?" She practically bounced up and down in her eagerness to help.

"I'm honestly not sure what I need. Is your mommy around?"

"Nope. She's upstairs working with clients. But I can help you!"

Erin glanced up the stairs before deciding to push onward. "I need something more to help with dreaming."

"Dreaming? Are you having bad dreams?"

"Not exactly. More like—I want to be able to control my dreams."

"Oh! My sister does that. You should talk to her."

"Your sister? Does she work here?" asked Erin.

The girl laughed. "Work here! That's a good one." She peeked behind a short bookcase that formed a small nook next to a window. "You don't work at all, do you?"

Erin looked over the bookcase.

An even smaller girl sat on the floor behind the bookcase, curled up with a large pile of picture books. She wore an oversized sequined gown, a feather boa shot through with tinsel, a rhinestone crown, and socks with high heels. "I do so!" She stood up from her little nook and put her hands on her hips.

"Then help this lady out, will you? She needs some dreaming equipment."

"Can you help me?" said Erin, somewhat dubious.

The tiny girl eyed Erin critically. She tossed her hair, clip-clopped over to the cash register, and picked up a shopping basket without saying a word. She stamped briskly through the shop, tossing in items seemingly at random, until she came to a stop in front of Erin. She pushed the basket into Erin's hands with a shy smile, then spun on her heel and returned to her reading nook.

"That's my sister," said the older girl cheerfully. She held the basket up for Erin's inspection. "*Lucid Dreaming for Beginners.* Amethyst, moonstone, Herkimer diamond, and moldavite. And a dream diary to write everything down."

"You think this will work?"

The girl shrugged. "Works for her. She has the best dreams."

Erin accepted the basket, and with it, the guidance of a pair of precocious children who appeared to run a magic shop all by themselves.

20

Erin curled up with Nancy Drew and a hot mug of tea to re-read *Lucid Dreaming for Beginners* one more time from cover to cover as the day faded into night. A pile of colorful sticky note pads sat close at hand. Occasionally, she'd peel off another sticky note and stick it on a pertinent page. She'd been jotting down notes in the dream diary for days, filling page after page with a teacher's neat handwriting.

The most fascinating section of *Lucid Dreaming for Beginners*, other than the practical part about how to start dreaming lucidly, was the part about how to tell if you were in a dream or reality. Erin amused herself with repetitions of the finger test, in which she pressed one finger into the palm of her other hand to try to make her finger pass through her palm. Of course, it wouldn't work in reality—but by creating the habit during her waking hours, she would remember to do it while dreaming. The finger test would serve to make her aware of being in a dream state.

Once in a while, she'd change it up and attempt a different reality check, like glancing at the clock twice to see if the time drastically changed between each glance, or placing one hand on the wall to check its solidity. The seemingly nonsensical actions were just silly enough to lift her spirits.

Picking up on Erin's mood, Nancy Drew playfully nudged Erin, her book, and anything else within Nancy's nearsighted range of vision.

"You're a good dog, Nancy," said Erin, ruffling the dog's silky ears. "We'll get the hang of this."

Tonight she would attempt to channel her newfound skills into a dream about Andy.

She prepared for bed by following sleep hygiene practices: skipping caffeine and alcohol, leaving the television off, and winding down with a warm bath. Later, when she began to yawn, she placed her new crystals and dream diary within easy reach on her nightstand.

When at last her eyelids became heavy with the need for rest, she slipped under the comforter and rested her head on the pillow. One at a time, she held each crystal against her forehead and concentrated on her intention before setting the crystal carefully back on the nightstand. She would practice her reality checks, seek insight on Andy's whereabouts, and—most importantly—remember her dreams. After consideration, she kept the quartz crystal necklace in place around her neck.

As she lay in bed with her eyes closed, she allowed herself to relax while gently holding on to the awareness of being awake. Images formed and dissolved behind her eyelids as her consciousness teetered back and forth between the state of wakefulness and the state of sleep.

Then there was nothing, and a sense of time passing.

She found herself in the coffee shop again. Erin looked around. She was supposed to meet Genevieve. She started toward the counter to order coffee, then noticed she already had a mug in her hands. Why was she here again? Hadn't she already done this?

Her gaze traveled over the coffee shop. Moments ago, it had been full of people. Now it was empty. Disorientation shuddered through her. She looked down, and the coffee mug she'd been holding in her hands seconds before was gone.

Slowly, she pressed one finger into the palm of her other hand. When her hand stretched like taffy, painlessly but with a uniquely discomforting sensation, her excitement nearly popped the dream like a floating soap bubble. She managed to calm herself just in time to maintain the dream state.

As she spun around to look for the door, the coffee shop disappeared entirely, to be replaced by her own living room. Her intentions faded under a haze that settled heavily on her thoughts. She was home. What was she doing at home? Where was Nancy Drew?

The house remained silent, lacking even the sound of Nancy's skittering paws. Erin realized all over again that she was still dreaming. Holding that thought firmly, Erin walked through the house. Andy's posters, which she had taken down days ago, hung throughout the house. The groceries he had purchased lay on the counters, untouched, while the full meal he had cooked from those groceries also sat improbably on the table as if waiting for her to sit down to eat.

In the bedroom, she found her little black dress laid out on the bed. Erin reached out one hand to touch the dress, but as soon as she did, she found that it wasn't on the bed at all.

She was wearing it.

Erin walked to the front door and opened it. In mid-swing, it became a sliding automatic door opening to the fancy grocery store where she and Andy had been shopping. Alongside the groceries, boxes of crystals and wands littered the shelves, interspersed with bottles of Champagne.

Curious, Erin picked up a bottle and examined the ornate label. The words read "Le Nouveau Palmier," until a second glance revealed them to be meaningless swirls.

The bottle slipped from her hands and struck the floor with a shattering crash. A splash of cold droplets of liquid obscured her vision, and she closed her eyes as the grocery store blurred into nothing.

When she opened them again, the grocery store was gone, replaced by the bare walls of her old classroom. Erin remembered—in a fuzzy, distant kind of way—that the room was not, in fact, completely empty of its furniture. In this dream state, however, it contained nothing at all.

Well, almost nothing.

Erin drew closer to a single object located on the floor in the center of the room. Whatever it was, it trembled in a nonexistent breeze. She knelt with her hand out. Her fingers closed around a soft gray feather flecked with white. She stood and brought the feather to her cheek, feeling the sensation as it traced the line of her cheekbone, the curve of her cheek, and finally her lips.

She smiled.

Holding the feather, she spun in a circle, just as she'd practiced, concentrating on her intentions as the room whirled away into nonexistence.

She opened her eyes to a heavy wooden bookshelf labeled "200" for the Dewey Decimal System, and immediately recognized her location as the school library. Although the silent darkness gave her pause, she gripped the feather more firmly and walked out of the shelves. She almost tripped on an abandoned picnic basket.

Sidestepping the basket, she entered the open seating area to be confronted with an unusual sight.

A white door floated without support in the middle of the room.

Erin approached it carefully. Why would there be a door in the middle of the library? Erin reached out and gingerly placed her hand on the door, finding it cool and smooth to the touch, with no handle or knob to be seen.

A scrap of Scripture came to mind. She spoke it aloud: "Ask, and it will be given to you; seek, and you will find; knock, and it will be opened to you." With that, she gripped the feather in one hand, and with the other, formed a fist and knocked on the door, belatedly realizing she'd used the rhythm of the "Ride of the Valkyries" just like her mother.

PART II
ANDROMALIUS

21

There were only a few decorations on the wall, and in his time stuck in the Waiting Room, Andromalius had stared at them all. There was the framed "No One Is Coming to Save You" sampler, cross-stitched with inexpertly formed flowers and vines. Then there was the faded "Hang In There" kitten poster, which could have been considered relatively inoffensive if it weren't for the fact that if he stared too long at the kitten, it gave the unnerving impression of staring back.

The only other decorative item—if it could be called decorative—was the worn-down "Take A Number" stand, which dispensed little green slips of paper with numbers that were never called.

Andy shifted in his chair, which seemed to have been designed for maximum discomfort, then stood up and charged the service window one more time. "Excuse me," he said to the woman-shaped creature occupying the booth. "Any estimate on when I can get out of here?"

The Waiting Room attendant—who, as a fellow supernatural being, could have appeared in any form in the known universe but chose to look like a slightly more severe version of Margaret Thatcher—didn't even look up from her pile of paperwork. "Has your number been called?" she asked without interest.

"You know damn well it hasn't," said Andy.

"Can't process your release until your number's been called."

"You haven't called any numbers in the last thousand years!" shouted Andy.

She ignored him and stamped a form with thick, rust-colored ink.

Andy kicked the front of the booth out of sheer pique, then strode over to the kitten poster. "I'm on to you," he said, pointing a finger at the kitten.

The kitten's whiskers might have twitched—but then again, maybe not.

Andy flung himself down in one of the many chairs. He'd sat in all of them since he'd been blasted out of earthly existence by that library witch. There was no way to tell how long it had been.

He'd been stuck in the Waiting Room various times over the millennia, for various reasons (some better than others). Each time, he could do nothing to set himself free. He could only wait for the Powers That Be to release him on their own mysterious schedule.

Andy sighed, pulled out his pocket notebook, and flipped through the pages for what seemed like the thousandth time. He'd had such a good thing going. He'd managed to get summoned by a mortal with a need for revenge and a hidden desire for vegetarian food. He'd felt useful for once, instead of knocking around the universe like an aging trust-fund kid with no place to call home.

Now he was stuck in the Waiting Room.

Andy leaned back and closed his eyes. Not for him, the blessed relief of sleep. No, he would experience every stultifying moment in all its tedious glory, with only an ersatz Maggie Thatcher to keep him company.

A rhythmic banging sound interrupted his self-pity.

Was it the "Ride of the Valkyries"?

Andy bolted up, stuffing his notebook in his pocket as he ran to the featureless white door of the Waiting Room. He pressed his hands against the door. "Someone's knocking," he called to the Waiting Room attendant.

She didn't look up.

He crossed the room to the booth and leaned down to the opening that allowed his voice to pass through the thick plexiglass-like material of the booth. He cleared his throat. "I said, someone is knocking on the door. To the rhythm of the 'Ride of the Valkyries,' to be precise."

"It's a funny old world," she muttered, still without looking up, but her hand darted below the desk.

A loud buzzing noise rang through the room.

Andy bolted to the door and pushed.

The door gave way and he stumbled through, quickly unfurling his wings to recover his balance. The Waiting Room disappeared in a blinding flash of white light.

Andy looked up.

Erin stood before him in a black cocktail dress, with an expression of shock that metamorphosed into a delighted smile. But when he started forward, her form faded away like fog.

Andy recognized a dream when he saw one, and—unlike the Waiting Room—dreams provided an easy path back to reality. Full of determination, he concentrated on shifting from the dream back to reality. He closed his eyes and moved without moving, following the breadcrumbs of Erin's subconscious all the way back to the real world.

Andy materialized in Erin's bedroom with a soft sigh of relief. His gaze traced Erin's form. She was still sleeping, her brown hair splayed over the pillow in nocturnal disarray, one foot poking out from the covers. Perhaps she dreamt on, or perhaps she had eased into a deeper sleep without dreams.

He carefully covered her foot with the comforter, then folded away his wings and tiptoed out of the room. "Don't wake her," he said to Nancy Drew outside the bedroom.

The dog cocked her head as if she understood.

After sunrise, Andy could wait no longer. He put the coffee on to brew and retrieved two mugs from the cabinet, remembering to move carefully so that he didn't startle her out of her wits by breaking a dish like he had the first time.

He sat down at the kitchen table and tried to pretend he had all the patience an immortal being should have.

He lasted thirty seconds before springing up and pacing the floor with silent footsteps.

Nancy Drew sat on the tile and turned her head back and forth to follow his movements.

The coffee maker burbled and hissed as it finished brewing.

Andy heard a rustle of fabric from the direction of the bedroom. He froze.

"Andy?" Erin's sleep-roughened voice drifted into the kitchen.

He hustled to the bedroom door but didn't open it. "Erin?" he said softly.

She opened the door, still in her pajamas, and rubbed her eyes before focusing her gaze on his face. "Are you really here?" She took a step back and poked her index finger forcefully into the palm of her other hand.

He watched this odd gesture with fascination. "What are you doing?"

"I'm making sure I'm awake."

Andy chuckled. "You're definitely awake. I promise."

"Prove it," she said.

"Follow me," he said. He returned to the kitchen and poured a mug of coffee, adding a bit of cream and two spoonfuls of sugar.

Erin watched him.

He held out the coffee. When Erin wrapped her hands around the warm mug, Andy placed his hands over hers. "Does this seem real to you?"

Erin met his gaze. "Very real."

He released her. "Well, then. Drink up."

She took a slow sip. "It's good."

"It should be. I made it," he said.

"And so modest, too." The corner of her mouth lifted in a playful smile. "I see you managed not to break anything this time."

He couldn't stop looking at her little smile, and the way it made her eyes crinkle at the corners, so he filled another mug with coffee to give himself a reason to look away. "There's always tomorrow."

22

Andy sat in the passenger seat of the car and crossed his arms. This seemed like a very bad idea.

"Come on, it'll be fine," said Erin. She placed a hand on his arm. "It was really hard to shop while talking to someone who wasn't there."

"I was there," said Andy, splitting hairs in order to stall what appeared to be the inevitable conclusion of Erin getting her way.

"Okay, fine." Erin used the hand on his arm to give him a little push. "You were there, but you were invisible. It was awkward."

Andy caved, like he knew he would. "Do I look okay?"

She looked him up and down. "Of course. You always look good. I'm envious," she teased.

"Envious? Of me? That's one of the seven deadly sins. Keep up the good work." He hopped out of the car.

She joined him. "You're supposed to compliment me back, you know. That's how this works."

"Oh, am I? I'm a little rusty. Hang on. Let me think." He faced her and struck a pensive pose. "I think you look beautiful when you get out of bed in the morning with mussed hair and wrinkled pajamas. How's that?"

Erin's cheeks turned pink. "That's...fine."

They walked through the parking lot to the grocery store entrance.

"Did I do it right?" Andy worried that he'd said something wrong.

"You should probably keep practicing."

"Then let me tell you about your eyes—"

"Maybe not right now."

"Oh," Andy said. "Right." He retrieved a cart.

They were halfway through the grocery store when a familiar voice trilled through the air.

"Erin, darling! What are you doing here?"

Erin's mother, Joyce, stood behind them in the wine aisle.

Andy put down a bottle before he dropped it out of pure panic.

"Hi, Mom," said Erin, moving to intercept her mother before she reached Andy. "This isn't your usual grocery store."

Joyce dodged Erin easily and confronted Andy. "And who's this?"

Should he turn invisible on the spot? No, it would probably just make things worse.

"I'm Andy," he said brightly.

"Andy?" Joyce looked to Erin for confirmation or explanation.

"Andy is my—" Erin stepped to Andy's side and threaded her arm through his. "Boyfriend. Yes. Andy is my boyfriend, Mom."

"Your boyfriend?" Joyce looked back and forth between Erin and Andy. "You never mentioned a boyfriend." Her eyes narrowed at Andy.

Andy bared his teeth in what he hoped was a friendly, open smile. "That's right. Erin is my *inamorata*."

Erin closed her eyes. It looked like she, too, wanted to turn invisible.

"Isn't that right, my love?" said Andy. He elbowed Erin discreetly.

"Are you from America?" asked Joyce.

"Yes," said Erin.

"No," said Andy, at the same time.

"I mean, yes, he's American, but he grew up overseas," said Erin.

"Really? Where?" said Joyce.

Andy felt Erin staring at him. "France," he said. In a fit of inspiration, he took Joyce's hand and bowed over it. "*Enchantée, madame.*"

Joyce slowly pulled back her hand. "I see. Well, this is certainly exciting. Will you be coming to church this Sunday, Erin? You could bring your new"—she paused to look Andy up and down—"boyfriend."

"I think we might go to his church this weekend," said Erin.

Andy's eyes widened at Erin's audacity.

"Oh? What church is that?" said Joyce.

"The church of—" Erin glanced frantically at Andy.

"Of—" said Andy.

"Yes?" prompted Joyce.

Andy said the first string of vaguely appropriate words that popped into his head. "The Church of the Sacred Heart of Our Lady of the—"

"Sea," finished Erin. "The Church of the Sacred Heart of Our Lady of the Sea."

If Joyce's eyebrows went any higher, they would have climbed off the top of her head and run away. "Never heard of it. Catholic, then?"

"Yes," said Andy firmly. "Exactly."

Joyce nodded. "Why don't you stop by the house afterward for lunch? Since you're shopping, you can pick up something to bring."

Andy and Erin looked at each other. Andy couldn't read Erin's pleading expression clearly enough to determine whether she wanted him to accept or decline Joyce's invitation, so he winged it. "Of course we'll come. I'll bring my famous devil's food cake."

"Oh, you bake?" said Joyce.

It didn't sound like a complimentary remark. Andy felt a rebellious impulse of mischief coming on. "I do bake," he said.

"Well, then," said Joyce. "I'll see you Sunday."

Andy and Erin stood together, their arms still linked, until Joyce turned down another aisle.

"What were you thinking?" whispered Erin. "Now we have to go to her ridiculous lunch!"

"I'm not the one who started a new relationship in the middle of a grocery store," said Andy.

Erin pressed her hand against her forehead. "I panicked!"

"Not hard to do around your mother," he said.

She hit him in the arm. "My mother is a saint."

"Your mother thinks she's a saint. There's a difference."

Erin snorted with suppressed laughter. "All right, truce. Mistakes were made. At least I get some devil's food cake out of it."

Andy leaned down to her ear and whispered, "I put the 'devil' in devil's food cake," and had the pleasure of bringing another smile to her lips.

23

After Erin fell asleep that night, Andy slipped out of the house and winged his way to his favorite overlook in the area. The 29-story condo building towered over the beachside peninsula, with a clear 360 degree view perfect for contemplation.

Unseen on the roof of the building, he stared out across the ocean waves dappled with moonlight. As an immortal, it was all too easy to become jaded, but Andy held on to an eternal optimist's sense of wonder. He closed his eyes and felt the humid air blow over his face and ruffle the feathers in his wings.

An English-accented voice rang out behind him. "Thought I'd find you here."

Andy turned his head. "Phoenix," he said. "How'd you know I'd be here?"

"On top of the tallest landmark in the area?" Phoenix shrugged, the motion rippling his glossy red wings in the moonlight. "Of course you'd be here."

"You're not wrong," said Andy. "What brings you out in the middle of the night?"

"Same as you, I assume. Escaping your assigned mortal."

Andy chuckled. "I don't know if I'd put it that way."

"I would. You have no idea what that witch, Raya, has put me through. Like I'm some kind of errand boy. You're lucky you escaped." Phoenix sat down next to Andy. "Speaking of escaping, how did you get back, anyway?" asked Phoenix.

"Your witch didn't tell you?"

"No, she just made a sarcastic remark about how you had already turned up, no thanks to me, and just like that"—he snapped his fingers—"I was free. So I went looking for you. Are you still bound to yours?"

"My what?"

"Your mortal. Erin?"

Andy rubbed his bearded chin. "In a manner of speaking."

"What the hell is that supposed to mean?"

"I'm supposed to help her get revenge on her jerk of an ex-husband."

"Well, that's easy. Go make his hair fall out or something, and you're done. Free as a bird!" said Phoenix.

"I made his pants fall off in front of his church congregation, but it wasn't as satisfying as I hoped it would be. At least, Erin didn't seem satisfied."

"She wanted more?"

"I don't know. It's like she wanted something different."

Phoenix rolled his eyes. "Mortals. They never know what they want."

"I don't want to leave until I do the job right," said Andy.

"You have too much of the angel in you, my friend," said Phoenix.

Andy raised his eyebrows. "How can you say that? I lie, I desecrate churches with my very presence, and I'm no stranger to temptation. I'm a better demon than you are, by far. Your last customer, might I add, described you as 'worthless.'"

Phoenix rubbed his hands together. "Oh, ho! Let's rewind a bit, shall we? Tell me more about this 'temptation.' Are you tempting this mortal?" His dark eyes shone.

Andy looked away.

"Come on, you can't lie to a brother demon. Tell Phoenix all about it."

Andy resisted the urge to shove Phoenix off the building. "I'm not tempting her."

"Leading her on only to crush her heart in the end?"

"Back off, Phoenix," said Andy.

Temporarily stunned into speechlessness, Phoenix looked Andy up and down. He clucked his tongue. "What have you gotten yourself into, mate?"

"Nothing," said Andy.

"Sitting there like a brooding hen? Don't tell me it's nothing."

Andy refused to speak.

Phoenix spoke more gently, for a demon. "You know nothing like that can work. You're immortal. She's not. There are no happy endings."

"I know that," said Andy. Pain bubbled up from whatever passed for his soul. "I don't want to talk about it."

"Suit yourself," said Phoenix. He pointed a finger at Andy. "But don't come crying to me when it blows up in your face."

"I can see why the witch said you were useless."

"Oh, very funny," said Phoenix.

"Actually, you can be of some use. How about helping me get some more revenge on this mortal I'm after?"

"Now that sounds like something right up my alley. What did you have in mind? We can't murder him, you know. It's against the rules. Sadly."

Andy shook his head. "No murder. But I'll take sheer terror."

"I like it," said Phoenix. "Phoenix and Andromalius, the team of terror." He spread his hands before him like a film director framing a shot.

"Like you said, we can't actually harm him. Physically. But"—here he flashed a grin—"there's no saying we can't make him think he's in serious trouble."

"You know, I can't say I understand your work ethic, but even I can appreciate your dedication to the craft." Phoenix leveled a small bow in Andy's direction.

"Thank you," said Andy.

"He seems like a right bastard, anyway," said Phoenix.

Both demons looked out across the water in silence, their wings hunched behind their backs.

Andy stood. "I should go."

"I think I'll stay here a while," said Phoenix. "I'm going to think of horrible things to do to her ex-husband."

"Good. I need some fresh ideas. Will you meet me here again tomorrow night?"

"Let me check my calendar." Phoenix pretended to page through an imaginary calendar. "As a matter of fact, I seem to be free for—oh, the next millennium." He closed the imaginary calendar and cocked his head at Andy.

Andy smiled, unfurled his wings, and flew into the night.

24

The smell of freshly baked chocolate cake filled the house. Andy smoothed chocolate frosting onto the cooled cake layers, lost in the meditative motions of baking.

Nancy Drew sat on her haunches and watched from a short distance away.

"No chocolate for you, doggo," said Andy.

Nancy sneezed.

"That's right. Dogs are allergic to chocolate." In lieu of cake, Andy tossed the dog a biscuit.

Erin walked into the kitchen. "Are there free samples?"

"Not for her. But for you, I might be persuaded."

"Please?"

"All right, I'm persuaded," said Andy. He scooped up frosting on a spoon and pressed it into a small pile of cake trimmings. "Here you go." He presented the spoonful of frosting and cake.

"That was easy," said Erin. "I hardly had to persuade you at all." She winked at him, then popped the spoon into her mouth.

Andy watched as she sampled the chocolate cake and frosting. Her eyes closed, and she smiled. "Chocolate heaven."

"It's devil's food cake, you know," he said.

"I know. But 'chocolate hell' just doesn't have the same ring to it."

"Devilishly good, then?" said Andy.

"Devilishly." She held out the spoon, which had been thoroughly licked clean.

As he took the spoon, his fingers brushed hers by accident. Had she noticed? Had she held eye contact just a little longer? Flustered, Andy turned away to put the spoon in the sink.

"I'm going to go finish getting ready," said Erin. She retreated to the bedroom and closed the door.

Andy closed his eyes. He hadn't felt like this in years.

Hundreds of years.

He opened his eyes and grabbed a second spoon, then hastily scooped up a large dollop of frosting and popped it into his mouth.

Even an overload of chocolate didn't help.

Erin peeked out the bedroom door. "Andy?"

Andy, his mouth full of frosting, could barely respond. "Mm?"

"What are you wearing to lunch?"

He swallowed the frosting hastily. "Let me see your outfit first."

She closed the door again.

Andy leaned on the counter and tried to clean the errant frosting from his mustache. He didn't have to have a mustache and beard, after all, or salt-and-pepper hair, or a red suit and bow tie. He could have appeared any way he wanted to, but a solid identity kept him from going completely mad over the years.

A solid identity, and frequent helpings of good chocolate and coffee.

When Erin emerged, she twirled before him. Her tropical print dress spun prettily with plenty of movement in the full skirt.

"Well?" she said.

"Devilishly beautiful," he said.

"Aren't men supposed to say, 'You look like an angel'?"

"I'm not a man," said Andy. "And besides, angels don't know the slightest thing about looking good."

She rolled her eyes. "Demons are the experts?"

"Undisputed." He gave her ensemble another look, then concentrated as he ran his hands down his body as he had done before when they went to Erin's school together.

Her eyes widened as his attire changed from his preferred chambray-and-denim work clothing combo to a casual suit the color of papyrus.

He turned in a slow circle with his arms extended. "How's this? I tried to go with the tropical look."

"It's…very nice," she said, still looking him up and down. "We'll look like a matched set."

"Really? Can I see?"

They went to the mirror together. Erin stood in front, with Andy behind and slightly to the side.

"We do look like a matched set," he said, pleased.

Erin's gaze took in their appearance, then shifted and caught his gaze in the mirror. "I hope I didn't make you uncomfortable with my mom at the grocery store. I didn't know what else to do."

"What, calling me your boyfriend? It's a high compliment." Andy carefully arranged a few of Erin's tresses to fall to the front.

Erin stilled his hand by touching it. "You're sure?"

"Positive. And besides, it's not like I have anything else to do."

She smacked his hand. "You—"

"Kidding!" He raised his hands in surrender. "Let's go, or we'll be late."

They left the house and got in Erin's car.

Andy, who would have preferred to fly invisibly to any given destination, buckled his seatbelt and felt very human. "So, what else should I—your boyfriend—know about you?"

"I think I need to know more about you. We established that you were both foreign and American simultaneously," said Erin, backing out of the driveway.

"*Mais oui*. It's actually true, though, if you think about it."

"Oh?"

"I lived in France for years."

Erin's face took on a dreamy look. "I'd love to go there."

"We should go. I know all the best places. At least, the ones that are still there."

"Still there?" said Erin.

"It was a while back," said Andy.

"I keep forgetting how old you are. How does that work, anyway? Were you here for the big bang?"

"It's fuzzy," he said. "I don't remember anything before humans came along."

"Sounds like you're too old for me," said Erin, with a sideways glance and a teasing smile.

Andy attempted a smile, but feared it would look pained, so he looked out the window and changed the subject. "So how did we meet?"

Erin's brow furrowed as the car came to a stop at a stoplight. "We met through a mutual friend?"

"Which one?"

"Raya would be the obvious choice."

Andy nodded. "Good thinking. How long have we been together?"

"A few months?" Erin accelerated when the light changed.

"What do we like to do together?"

"Making posters, making and/or eating cake, and taking long walks with an old dog," said Erin.

"What do you like about me?" said Andy.

Erin hit the brakes sharply. "Sorry. Thought I saw a squirrel." She seemed rattled. "I like a lot of things about you. Cake, for one."

Andy laughed.

"And your enthusiasm for things. And your cooking skills."

"And my massage skills," added Andy.

"And your modesty," said Erin. "What about me? Why are you 'dating' me?"

"I like your dog," said Andy.

"What?"

"Wait, that came out wrong. I mean that I like how you care for Nancy Drew. How you care about your job teaching little mortals. You care about everyone. You even cared enough about me to come looking for me."

"Anyone would have done that," said Erin.

"Not just anyone would have even tried, and even fewer would have succeeded. And I like how you're open to new things and willing to take a chance even when you've been hurt."

Erin's fingers gripped the wheel. "That's—very specific."

"I didn't offend you, did I? Oh, I've said the wrong thing!"

"Not at all," said Erin. "I just wasn't expecting such a thoughtful response. I thought your reasons would be something like my hair, or my eyes."

"Would you like me to talk about those?"

"Maybe another time," said Erin.

"Are you sure? I don't mind practicing before we get there."

"I'm sure."

"What else will your mom want to know?"

Erin snorted. "Probably what kind of job you have."

"What kind of job do I have?" asked Andy.

"How about a translator?"

"*Parfait*. A freelance translator, who flies wherever he is needed. Literally."

"Okay. Be ready, though. My mother can be a little…difficult."

"Erin, I'm a demon. I've dealt with the most difficult beings in the universe."

Erin shook her head. "You only think you have."

25

Andy had never thought of a round dining table as a circle of Hell, but he was about to make an exception for this one.

"Andy, do your parents go to church?" said Erin's mother, Joyce.

"They're dead," said Andy, improvising wildly.

"Oh, I'm so sorry," said Joyce. She took a sip from her glass of iced tea before continuing. "But did they go to church?"

Andy was tempted to unfurl his wings and grow horns. That would put a stop to her intrusive line of questioning. He smiled, imagining her expression. Only then did he trust himself to answer. "It was in France. You wouldn't have heard of it."

"Mom, are there any more rolls?" said Erin.

"In a minute, honey. I'm talking to your boyfriend." Joyce said "boyfriend" with two distinctly drawn-out syllables.

Andy waited for the next salvo of questions while imagining bursting through the roof and flying away.

Far away.

"Young people today—"

"Mom, please—" said Erin.

"No, go on, Joyce," said Andy. He winked at Erin where Joyce couldn't see.

"As I was saying before I was so rudely interrupted"—she shot a look at Erin before continuing—"young people today just aren't as interested in the religion of their forefathers."

"Oh, but I am," said Andy, his eyes shining. "In fact, I've made a special study of demonology."

Erin made a choking noise.

"Really?" said Joyce. She leaned in. "Tell me about that."

"Well, from what I've read, they're positively everywhere."

"I've heard that," said Joyce. "Makes you wonder what they're up to."

Andy nodded solemnly. "It does."

"Mom? Rolls?" said Erin. "Remember?"

"I would love some rolls," said Andy. "May I help you in the kitchen, Joyce?"

"You may," said Joyce, pushing her chair back.

"I'll come," said Erin, leaping out of her seat.

"You sit," said Joyce. "We'll be right back."

Erin slowly lowered herself into the chair.

When Joyce's back was turned, Andy gave Erin an enthusiastic thumbs-up to show that he had everything completely under control.

In the kitchen, Andy pulled the rolls out of the warm oven while Joyce retrieved a platter from the cabinet. They stood side by side as Joyce carefully transferred the rolls one at a time from the hot pan to the platter.

"How much do you know about Erin's divorce?" asked Joyce.

Andy was caught flat-footed. "I—"

"Nevermind," said Joyce. "It doesn't matter. What does matter is that she got hurt pretty bad. She doesn't need to go through anything like that ever again. You see what I'm saying?"

When Joyce looked at Andy, her eyes reminded him of the many eyes of one of the more fearsome demonic creatures he had known. "I think so," he hazarded.

Her gaze turned even sharper. "I'm glad to hear it." With that, she picked up the platter and strolled into the dining room. "Rolls!" she said, trilling the "r" and leaning down to offer them to Erin first.

Andy followed her out and returned to his seat.

Erin piled several hot rolls onto her plate. "Thanks."

Joyce seated herself. "So, I assume you heard the news?"

"About the wedding?"

Joyce sat up straight with surprise. "You knew?"

Erin nodded. "Genevieve told me."

"She told you? I didn't think you two were even speaking."

"She asked to meet me in person to give me the news. I guess she thought it was right somehow."

Joyce gave Andy a sidelong glance before returning her gaze to Erin. "You're going, right?"

"Mom, why would I go to their wedding?"

"You should show that you're over him. Show him you're moving on. Stick it right in his eye with your handsome new boyfriend." Joyce nodded toward Andy. "Isn't that right, Andy?"

Andy realized his mouth was hanging slightly open. He closed it quickly and looked at Erin.

"Don't be ridiculous, Mom," she said.

"I'm not ridiculous, young lady. I think you should stand tall and hold your head high and show off Mr. GQ over here."

"I don't have anything to wear," muttered Erin.

"We can go shopping," said Joyce.

"I have to get ready for school."

"That's a lie. I know you already moved your classroom with this guy." She raised her eyebrows and pointed toward Andy.

Andy felt Erin's gaze even before he turned his own to meet hers.

"Andy?" said Erin. "What do you think?"

"I'll do whatever you want," said Andy, and he meant it even more than she knew.

"See? He's game," said Joyce. "Here's what you do: you get yourself a nice dress, pretty shoes, a new hairstyle, maybe a little makeup, and you waltz in with a good-looking young man on your arm."

"It's not exactly a vote of confidence if you think I need a complete makeover."

"Sure it is. Do it for you, not for him. Or her." Joyce helped herself to another roll.

"I hate to say it, but I'm kind of with your mom on this one," said Andy.

"Not you too?"

"I think you should do whatever makes you feel best—but you know I'm all for some living-your-best-life revenge."

Erin looked undecided.

"Come on," said Joyce. "Live a little. Cause a little ruckus. It'll be good for you."

"You're telling me to cause a ruckus? You, the mother who once told me to stop raising my hand so much in Sunday School because it made me look overeager?"

Andy choked and nearly spat out a mouthful of tea.

"See, look what you've done," said Joyce, whacking Andy firmly on the back.

Erin shook her head. "I'll never understand you."

"That's all right, honey. Children aren't meant to understand their parents. They should just listen to them and do everything they say," said Joyce, her delivery perfectly serious.

Andy watched the thoughts play across Erin's face like a chyron of emotions, passing from consternation to determination.

A mischievous smile slowly graced her lips.

"Guess we better go shopping, then," said Erin.

26

That night, Andy beat Phoenix to their pre-arranged meeting spot atop the tall condo building overlooking the water. Andy sat looking west over the intracoastal waterway, watching the evening star rise. Venus glowed in the clear sky, bright enough to outshine the true stars.

He felt the mantle of age settle over his shoulders like moonlight—always there, even if it couldn't be seen. How long had he looked up at the sky and watched the stars trace their paths?

A ruffle of feathers and a rush of air alerted Andy to the presence of Phoenix, who landed neatly and spoke without preamble. "Have I got some ideas for you."

Andy continued to stare at the sky.

"What, no hearty greeting? No 'Thank you, Phoenix, for coming up with brilliant ideas'?" Phoenix sat next to Andy. "Or even a 'Thank you for coming to sit on this godforsaken building when you could have been off doing something far more entertaining'?"

"I'm sorry," said Andy. "I just don't think it's going to work."

"What do you mean? We were going to get some really juicy revenge together, Andy. You're disappointing me. Where's your famous demon work ethic?"

"It's not what she wants."

"Who, Erin? Of course she wants revenge. She's only human," said Phoenix.

"She wants to move on, Phoenix."

"Oh. Oh, I see. So we're done here, then? I can go? Or, I should say—we can go?" Phoenix made as if to get up.

"You can go if you want," said Andy.

Phoenix rolled his eyes. "Oh, for the love of all that is unholy, Andy, what is your problem?"

Andy sighed. "Look, I can handle wickedness. I know how to get revenge. But what she wants now"—he raised his palms to the night sky like he was pleading—"how am I supposed to give her that?"

"The 'moving on' part?"

Andy nodded miserably.

"A wise chap of my acquaintance once said that living well is the best revenge."

"Don't quote my own words back at me," said Andy.

"Why not? It's you who needs to hear the damned things."

"How does that help me with Erin?"

"Are you that stupid?" said Phoenix. "You can still help her. Whether that includes terrorizing Mark, or making his hair fall out, or cancelling all his credit cards, or whatever mad scheme you came up with, you can find a way to make it fit in with what she wants. Help her live well."

"Help her live well," echoed Andy.

"It's so obvious. You're the Finder of Lost Things, right?"

"Yes…"

"Well, act like it, Andromalius! When her ex-husband put her through the wringer and left her high and dry—"

"That's a terrible mixed metaphor," Andy said.

"Shut up and listen. When that happened, she lost something. Something important."

"What's that?"

"That's what you need to find out. Help her find what she lost. Can I spell it out for you any more clearly?"

"How did you become wise, Phoenix?"

"Years of recklessness followed by inevitable consequences," said Phoenix.

"Makes sense."

The two demons stared at the night sky.

"How does she feel about you, anyway?" said Phoenix.

Andy smoothed his beard nervously. "I don't know. She likes me."

"And you like her. Except—it's a little more than that, isn't it?"

As a demon who had long ago learned to set aside attachments, Andy had pretty much forgotten how to cry. Instead, his wings involuntarily shuddered.

"Bloody hell. You've got to get a hold of yourself, mate. We talked about this," said Phoenix.

"I know."

"It can't work. No human wants an ancient demon like you or me. Not for anything serious, anyway."

"I know," said Andy, holding his head in his hands.

"Even if you've mellowed with time and picked up a few skills here and there."

"I know!" cried Andy, startling a nearby vulture roosting on the roof.

"So why torture yourself?"

Andy laughed ruefully. "Torture is what demons do best."

"Besides, you may look male to her, but for supernatural beings, gender's just a habit. How's she going to take that?"

"You're killing me," said Andy.

"I wish I could. It'd put you out of your misery. Be a mercy, really."

"Thanks a lot."

"Any time," said Phoenix.

Andy shifted slightly before changing the subject. "She's supposed to go out tomorrow. With Raya."

"Not the witch again?"

"To go shopping for a makeover," said Andy.

"Shopping for a makeover?" Phoenix scoffed. "Raya wouldn't know a dress from a hole in the ground. All she ever wears are pithy t-shirts and jeans."

"I'll be there."

Phoenix waved Andy's remark away. "You'll be too busy making puppy dog eyes to talk sense."

"I resent that," said Andy, ruffling his wing feathers in indignation.

"You resemble it," countered Phoenix. "No, I'll have to go. Someone has to take charge of you lot. Bunch of hapless mortals and a lovesick demon."

"What will Raya think if you show up?"

"What do I care? She can bloody well deal with it," said Phoenix, hunching his wings and unintentionally making himself look like a petulant gargoyle. "Where are we going, anyway?"

"I was thinking—the mall?" Even as Andy said it, he cringed, anticipating Phoenix's reaction.

"The mall? That's all you could come up with?"

"It's not like I can fly her to Paris."

"Well, technically, you could."

"Not on this short notice, and not without a lot of awkward questions."

"Fine, fine. The mall it is." Phoenix made a face of distaste. "Stuck in a backwater and condemned to go to the mall. That's what I get for getting mixed up with you."

"Thank you, Phoenix," said Andy.

Phoenix edged away. "Don't get all mushy on me."

Andy held up his hands in surrender. "I won't."

Phoenix huffed. "See that you don't."

They lapsed into companionable silence—two demons with all the time in the world—as the rising moon illuminated the river from edge to edge.

27

The four doors of Erin's sedan slammed one after another as Raya, Erin, Andy, and Phoenix stepped out of the car and into the parking lot of the local mall.

The mall had seen better days. Years of rain had left rusty trails running down the sides of the exterior. Birds nested in the parking lot lights, and scruffy grass overran the concrete planters.

Phoenix inhaled deeply. "Ah, you can smell the decline."

"Smells like capitalism to me," said Raya.

Erin approached Andy. "We were going to practice looking like a couple, right?"

Andy started. "Right! Yes. Let's do that." He held one hand out gingerly, as if testing a pan on the stove to see how hot it was.

Erin placed her hand softly in his. "See? I don't bite."

They walked into the first department store.

"Oh, look at this!" Raya skipped over to a nearby rack and picked up a sleek little black dress.

"Don't be ridiculous," said Phoenix, taking the dress out of her hands and returning it to the rack. "It's a wedding, not a funeral."

"I like black," said Raya. "Shoot me."

"If only," said Phoenix.

"Fine, no black. How about this?" Raya darted away and picked up a white lace cocktail dress.

Erin made a skeptical face. "I think it would draw attention if someone other than the bride was wearing white."

"You have to admit, it'd be funny," said Raya. She laid the dress against herself. "How do I look?"

"Unconvincing," said Phoenix.

Raya stuck out her tongue at him and dropped the hanger onto the rack with a clang.

Andy kept holding Erin's hand and turned to face her. Was she blushing? He couldn't tell. "Erin, what do you like to wear? What's your favorite color?"

"I like pink," she said.

"Pink it is, then," said Andy. He turned to Phoenix and Raya. "Stop messing around, and find the lady something pink."

"Yes, oh Great Earl," said Phoenix. He bowed to Andy, then threw his arm around Raya and said, "Let's go."

She immediately punched him in the gut.

Phoenix doubled over. "Ow!"

"Something wrong, Phoenix?" Raya said as she sauntered away.

Phoenix went after her, calling "I was just trying to be friendly!"

Erin looked at Andy. "They're quite a pair." She smiled.

"A very weird pair," said Andy. He reveled in the gentle pressure from her hand and had to stop himself from giving it an affectionate squeeze.

He couldn't forget that all of this boyfriend and girlfriend play-acting was only a charade. Andy fled from that line of thought and focused on the present. Here and now, he held Erin's hand. She had smiled at him.

It would have to be enough.

"How about this one?" said Andy. He used his free hand to pick up a pink dress with a full skirt.

"Too floofy."

He set it down. "This one?" He picked up a sleeker style with cutouts on the sides.

"Too revealing."

Andy put it back.

"Is that noise coming from Raya and Phoenix?" said Erin.

Andy followed her gaze across the store to see them standing toe to toe, having a shouting match that was unintelligible at that distance. "We'd better get them." He let go of Erin's hand as they speed-walked to the arguing pair.

"You look more like a couple than we do," said Erin.

That stopped Raya and Phoenix in mid-argument.

"We had to stop practicing holding hands just to run over here and interrupt your lovers' quarrel," added Andy, giving Phoenix a particularly hard look.

"Did you just call this a lovers' quarrel?" said Raya. "I'll have you know this idiot told me I didn't know a thing about clothes."

"Well, you don't—" Phoenix began, then stopped when he caught the look on Andy's face. "I mean, you're too busy with all the really important things you do to worry about something as superficial as fashion."

Raya stared at him suspiciously. "Like what important things?"

"Like…library things. And"—here he lowered his voice—"really powerful magic."

"You think so?" She looked ever so slightly mollified.

"I know so," said Phoenix, for once pouring his charm in Raya's direction.

Andy felt Erin slip her hand back into his and tried not to sigh with happiness.

They moved through the racks as a foursome, picking up and discarding one dress after another.

By lunchtime, they'd scoured three different department stores with no success. Raya and Erin, being the only ones in the group with a need to eat, declared a break for lunch and led the way to the food court.

"A food court?" Phoenix scowled.

Andy looked around hopefully. "Is there somewhere to get a good glass of wine?"

Erin laughed and hooked her arm through his. "You haven't been in food courts much, have you?"

"What are you having?" he asked.

"I think I'll go to the smoothie place," said Erin.

"That sounds tolerable," said Phoenix. "Given the situation."

"Oh, stop being such a stick-in-the-mud," said Raya. "I'll have one, too."

They carried their rainbow-hued smoothies to an unsteady table with four metal chairs and sat down.

"So, how's the whole pretending to be a couple thing going?" said Phoenix with wide, innocent eyes. "Ready to move on from just holding hands?"

Given the choice, Andy would have drowned Phoenix with his own smoothie. Instead, he looked daggers in his direction to try to get him to be quiet.

"What do you mean?" said Erin, looking up from her drink.

"You've held hands all morning. Is that all? Do you think that will sell it?" said Phoenix.

Erin's brow furrowed.

"It's fine," Andy said. "Phoenix, it's—"

"No," said Erin. "Phoenix has a good point. We should have a few more tricks up our sleeves."

"I knew I liked this girl!" said Phoenix, raising his smoothie to her.

"Really, Erin, you don't have to do anything you—" said Andy.

"We should kiss at least once," said Erin.

Andy, thunderstruck, looked from Erin, to Raya, and finally Phoenix.

Phoenix—damn him—grinned triumphantly.

"Good idea," said Raya, who was watching Erin across the table.

"See?" said Erin. "They like the idea." She paused and leaned closer to Andy, her face full of concern. "Unless you don't?"

Andy could smell the scent of her hair. "No, it's fine. I mean, I'm fine with it. If you are." His speech stumbled to a stop as he found it harder and harder to craft a coherent response.

"We can start with a kiss on the cheek," said Erin.

"Oh," said Andy, nonplussed.

Erin set her hand decisively on his jawline, drew him forward ever so slightly, and pressed her lips to his cheek. Her lips felt soft, and cool from the smoothie she'd been drinking.

The sensation sent shivers all the way to Andy's toes. His eyes closed.

"Well? How was that?" She was sitting back again, looking like the cat that got the cream.

Did she like the kiss? Was it even possible? Andy tamped down his hopes before he sprouted wings right there in the food court. He cleared his throat. "It was fine. Very good."

"I think you should kiss every time we go in a new store," said Raya. "For practice."

Phoenix nodded sagely. "Yes, for practice, Andy."

Erin raised her eyebrows at Andy. "You game?"

Andy, who was beginning to feel like he had been redeemed and sent to some sort of heaven, could only nod. He drank his smoothie as quickly as possible. "Ready when you are," he said when he finished.

28

The quartet approached the entrance to the last of the department stores. They had found nothing wedding-worthy at any of the preceding stores, and Andy, who had found the idea of kissing Erin to be heavenly, quickly discovered that in practice it was far more like Hell.

He couldn't abide the idea that Erin only went along with it because she wanted to put on a convincing show at her ex's wedding, but he also wanted to make her happy—and if that meant putting on a show, Andy would put on a show. It was a terrible position to be in. The fact that the kissing part was very nice just made it more like torture.

He steeled himself as he faced Erin.

"All right, you two, let's go," said Phoenix, gesturing meaningfully.

"On the lips this time," said Raya.

"What?" said Andy. Panicked, he shot Phoenix a look.

Phoenix returned the look with an innocent smile.

Andy's gaze switched to Erin.

She looked back at him with quiet expectation.

Well, then. If that's the way it had to be, then he would do it right. He took a firm step forward, closing the distance between them, and swept one arm around the small of her back. His other hand softly cradled Erin's head, her hair soft under his fingers.

Erin's head tilted slightly back and her lips turned upward at the corners.

Andy kissed her sweet smile and felt Erin's arms wrap around him, holding him in a state of bliss for what seemed to be eternity.

Raya slow-clapped and grinned at the two of them.

"Now that's a kiss," said Phoenix.

Erin drew back, pink at the cheeks.

Andy would have banished Phoenix—or murdered him, if it were possible—for interrupting. Instead, he turned back to Erin. "Was it okay?"

Erin cleared her throat. "It was great. I mean—it was fine."

"You're sure?"

She nodded.

Phoenix slapped him on the back. "You'll make a very convincing couple. Now let's find a damned dress and get out of here."

They proceeded into the store. The scent of the store's perfume counter wafted out in a melange of riotous aromas.

Andy nearly stumbled in the aisle, still reeling from the kiss, and now under assault by the overpowering perfume.

Erin slipped up beside him and took his hand. "Are you okay?"

"I'm fine," said Andy.

"You don't look fine," she said.

"I'm allergic to perfume."

"That can't even be possible."

Andy said nothing.

"Look, I'm sorry I roped you into this wedding date thing. If you're uncomfortable, we can call the whole thing off." She stopped and turned to face him in the aisle as Phoenix and Raya wandered further into the store.

He couldn't look her in the eye. "I'm just worried," he said.

"About what?"

"I'm worried that I won't do a good enough job for you."

Was she buying it?

Her gaze caught his. "Is that all? I think you're doing wonderfully. I couldn't ask for a better pretend boyfriend."

The double-edged compliment cut Andy like an angel's sword. "Thank you," he said.

They hurried to catch up with Raya and Phoenix, who were having a tug of war over a dress.

"This one is too short," said Raya.

"It's just the right amount of too short," said Phoenix.

Raya rolled her eyes. "You have no idea what you're talking about."

"Who makes these rules, anyway?" said Phoenix. "Too short. Wrong color. Too revealing. You mortals bedevil yourselves better than I ever could." He won the tug of war but dropped the dress on the rack with a look of exasperation.

"Children, children," said Andy, relieved to be in a situation in which he could maintain some semblance of control. "Stop fighting." He turned to Erin. "Honey, do you see anything you like?"

The other three stared at him.

"What?" said Andy.

"Honey?" said Raya.

"Oh, sweetie darling!" said Phoenix, elbowing Raya.

They both collapsed into snickers.

"I like it," said Erin, releasing Andy's hand and threading her arm through his in a gesture of apparent solidarity. "Darling," she added, bumping him playfully with her hip.

Andy beamed.

"Keep this up and you two are going to disgust everyone at that wedding," said Phoenix.

"That's the whole idea," said Erin. "Now can we focus?"

"How about this one?" said Raya. She lifted a dress from another rack and held it up.

"That's more like it," said Erin. She took the dress and held it up against herself. "I'm going to try this one on. Raya, will you help me zip up?"

The women left for the fitting room.

Phoenix turned to Andy and looked him up and down. "You're dying, aren't you?"

Andy shot Phoenix a look. "You're not helping."

Phoenix smirked. "Sure I am. You kissed her on the lips, didn't you?"

"I suppose I should thank you—for torturing me."

"I'm not torturing you. You're torturing yourself. You might as well loosen up and enjoy this while it lasts, you know."

"You're heartless."

"So are you, technically. Physicality is just an illusion."

"Go to Hell."

"For what? Telling you the truth?"

"I don't need you to tell me anything," said Andy.

"You're delusional," said Phoenix, shaking his head. "I'm just trying to stop you from making a fool of yourself."

Andy smiled sadly at his old friend. "Too late."

29

Nancy Drew skittered to the front door as it swung wide to allow Andy and Erin inside.

Erin held the dress aloft to keep it out of reach of the dog. "I'll put this away." She slipped past the dog and the demon, and headed for her bedroom.

Andy knelt in the entryway. "Hello, old girl." He patted the dog.

Nancy's cloudy eyes focused on his face.

"You're lucky your life is so uncomplicated," he said, smoothing his hand over her ears.

Nancy Drew wagged her tail.

"Immortality isn't all it's cracked up to be."

Erin's voice carried from the bedroom. "Andy, are you talking to the dog again?"

"Just a little," called Andy. He gave the dog a final pat and stood up. "I'm glad you found a dress you liked."

Erin walked out of the bedroom. "Me, too. I was beginning to think we'd run out of stores before I found one."

"Are you hungry? Can I make you something?"

"I'm okay." She ran her fingers over her hair. "On second thought, how about some cocoa?"

Andy followed her into the kitchen. "Where's your cocoa?"

Erin pulled a red canister out of a cabinet. "I got it."

Andy retrieved a small pot and brought it to the stove. "What else do we need?"

"Milk. Sugar and salt. And some vanilla." Erin took the milk out of the refrigerator and poured it, without measuring, into the pot.

Andy rummaged in the pantry for the rest of the ingredients. "Sugar, salt, and vanilla." He put each one on the counter within Erin's reach.

"Thanks." She spooned cocoa and sugar into the pot, following it with a pinch of salt and a spoonful of vanilla.

Andy held up a whisk he'd pulled from a drawer. "May I?"

She stepped back. "You may."

Nancy Drew, intrigued by the noise, joined them in the kitchen. She sat on her haunches and watched.

"Where'd you get this cocoa recipe?" asked Andy. He stirred the mixture slowly to incorporate the cocoa powder without sending it flying.

"My mom."

"Ah, the redoubtable Joyce." Andy whisked faster.

"I still feel bad about telling her you were my boyfriend."

"Oh? Why would you say that?" Andy attempted to keep a light tone.

Some of the liquid splashed out of the pot as he stirred.

"I put you on the spot."

"Nonsense. I would have done the same thing," said Andy.

Erin leaned against the counter. "You would have?"

"Well, not exactly, perhaps—I have neither a mother nor an ex-husband. But I can imagine that if I did, I would have done just what you did."

"It must be kind of lonely, being a demon." Erin turned away and took two mugs from the cabinet.

Andy shrugged. "You get used to it."

The cocoa began to steam.

"Here," said Erin. "Let me." She carefully poured the hot cocoa into two mugs, and handed him one.

Nancy Drew scratched at the back door.

Erin opened the door with one hand and followed the dog outside, into the night air.

Andy followed her.

They sipped from their mugs and looked at the night sky. The last light of the sun lingered in the west, sending up a faint glow beneath the blaze of the evening star.

"Have you ever thought about staying in one place for a while?" She was watching him.

He carefully avoided looking at her. "Sometimes."

"Do you get attached to people?"

The question sank into him like an arrow. "Even demons have feelings."

"That's not an answer."

Unable to look away any longer, he faced her. "Yes. I get attached. But it doesn't do anyone any good. Not me. Not the people I get attached to."

She calmly drank her cocoa. "Why's that?"

"Because—"

"Because it ends?"

"Yes," he said. He drank his cocoa to avoid having to say more.

Nancy Drew toddled around the backyard as fast as an old dog could toddle, happily sniffing and snuffling as she went.

They finished their cocoa in silence.

Erin took Andy's empty mug. "Everything ends, Andy. It's just a matter of time—and how you want to spend it." She whistled for the dog.

Nancy Drew attempted to run to Erin, but settled for ambling instead.

"Goodnight, Andy."

He wanted to reach for her just then, take the mugs from her hands and let them fall to the damp earth, wrap her up in his wings and let the moment last forever. Instead, he stepped aside to let her pass. "Goodnight. I'll come inside in a little bit," he added.

The door closed.

Andromalius unfurled his wings and shot into the sky. If he could just fly fast enough, he could leave himself behind. He surged higher and higher, the streetlights shrinking with distance as he pulled away from the ground and everything on it.

At the top of the arc of his flight, he hung in the air, orienting himself before plunging from the sky at a startling speed toward where he suspected he would find Phoenix.

―――⋅―――

Andy pounded on the door, ignoring the "Trespassers Will Be Cursed" sign.

A dog barked, then a female voice echoed from within the house. "Hold your horses."

The door opened. Raya leaned against the doorframe, attempting to restrain a large black dog who was trying its best to leap on Andy. "What are you doing here?"

"May I come in?" It paid to be polite to the witch who had enough raw power to send him hurtling back to the Waiting Room.

"Knock yourself out," she said, hauling the dog backwards to allow Andy to pass. "Don't mind Blaze. She's just a big old softie."

Andy eyed the dog, then entered to find Phoenix sprawled on Raya's couch. "Thought I'd find you here."

"You're just in time," said Phoenix. "We were going to play a board game."

Raya released Blaze, who bounded happily to Phoenix and laid her large head on his chest.

Andy's eyebrows shot up. "I thought you could barely be in the same room without arguing with or insulting each other."

"There will be plenty of insults, trust me. Isn't that right, you unscrupulous witch?"

"I'll crush you, spawn of Satan." She opened the Monopoly box and unfolded the board.

Andy looked from the witch to the demon and back again. He didn't have time for whatever this was.

"Phoenix, get up. We're leaving."

"What, now?"

"Yes, now."

"I don't want to." Phoenix pushed out his lower lip and pouted. "I want to play Monopoly."

"Phoenix…" Andy let the undertone of his voice slide into a range inaudible to humans.

Blaze jumped up and barked.

Phoenix rolled his eyes dramatically. "Don't threaten me, mate. I outrank you."

"Are you threatening him?" said Raya. A hard glint came into her eyes.

"No! I need his help. That's all."

Raya, somewhat mollified, returned to setting up the board game.

Phoenix sighed heavily and stood up. "I must postpone your thrashing for a later time," he said to Raya. "Will this take long, Andromalius?"

Andy shook his head.

"Fine. Let's go. I'll see you later, witch."

"Later, demon. Bye, Andy."

The two demons left by the front door.

Phoenix's red wings unfolded. He shot into the sky first, followed closely by Andy.

"What was that all about?" said Andy.

"What?"

"Don't play innocent demon with me. You're no good at it," said Andy as they flew side by side through the moonless night. "You gave me all that song and dance about not getting mixed up with mortals, and here you are cozying up for board game night with Raya?"

"It's just a lark," said Phoenix, rotating onto his back to stare up into the endless sky.

Andy snorted.

"I'm allowed to be hypocritical and inconsistent. I'm a demon," said Phoenix.

"No kidding."

"What do you want with me, anyway? Dragging me away from hearth and home in the dead of night—"

"Hearth and home? You're not inconsistent—you're insane! Since when did you call anywhere home?"

"It's just an expression," said Phoenix.

Andy felt more confused than ever. He tried to shake it off, literally shaking his wings in flight as if to shed loose feathers. "Let's pay a visit to Erin's ex."

"Will that make you less grumpy?"

"Maybe," said Andy, his face settling into grim lines.

"Did you discuss this with her, by any chance?"

"No."

"Brilliant," said Phoenix, meaning the exact opposite. "Of course, she doesn't want revenge any more." He pulled up short and froze in mid-air as the realization hit him. "But you do."

Andy, who had overshot Phoenix, spun around and covered the distance back to his fellow demon. "What does it matter? We're wasting time."

Phoenix's wings beat slowly. "We have all the time in the world. Why are you rushing into this?"

"Are you going to help me, or not?" Andy gained altitude and prepared to dive.

"When have I ever said no to revenge?"

Andy plunged from the sky, his outline tinged with fire, and Phoenix followed in his wake.

30

They settled unseen and unheard on the roof of Mark's house. Andy sensed the sleeping mortals without having to see them.

"How do you want to do this?" said Phoenix.

"Remember that time in Paris?"

Phoenix smiled fondly. "How could I forget?"

"Like that."

"Can I do that thing from Madrid, too?"

"Go for it," said Andy.

"I'll see you on the inside," said Phoenix, closing his eyes.

Andy closed his eyes and concentrated on the dreamers, his consciousness seeking out Mark like a homing missile. Awareness of the warm night faded away as he dropped into the mind of another being.

It was so rare that he had the opportunity to manifest himself creatively that he hardly knew where to start. He deepened his outline of fire until it blazed. He allowed two curving horns to protrude from his forehead. His teeth sharpened to points as his wings transformed from their neat salt-and-pepper coloration to a light-sucking shade of black.

Phoenix, on the other hand, dialed up the deep red velvet color of his wings to a lurid shade of crimson, and outlined himself in flickering black shadows. The irises and the white of his eyes were subsumed by darkness.

"No horns?" said Andy.

"Must I?"

"They expect it."

Phoenix sighed. "Fine." Spiraling ram's horns grew from his head. "I look bloody stupid."

Andy observed the effect. "Nonsense. You look terrifying."

"Great. Are we going with formal regalia, or more of a rag-and-bone look?"

Andy considered. "Formal's too good for this clown."

"So I get to look stupid and ugly. You're going to owe me for this, Andy."

"Just do it."

Arrayed in their best—or worst, depending on your point of view—outfits of soiled sackcloth, they faced the void of Mark's dreams.

"Where is he, anyway?" said Phoenix.

"In between dreams."

"Well, get him here and let's get this over with."

Andy concentrated, reached out, and pulled.

Mark appeared before them, wearing only a pair of boxer shorts and looking very confused.

It was time to raise the stakes.

"Mark." Andy's voice boomed like an avalanche of gravel.

"Mark," Phoenix echoed, his voice hissing like a pit of snakes.

Mark stumbled backwards in terror, then turned and ran.

The two demons grinned at each other and gave chase. It was too easy, given that Mark was confined to the logic of his own dream. They blocked his wild retreat and circled him, keeping him off-balance and trapped.

"What do you want?"

"We want you, Mark," said Andy, leaning into his role with as much menace as he could manage.

"We want your soul," said Phoenix, who appeared to be enjoying himself despite his earlier complaints.

"My soul?" Mark's voice cracked.

Andy loomed over Mark, who dropped to his knees and covered his face. "Your foul soul is tarnished with a thousand terrible sins, Mark. You cheated on your wife—"

"With her best friend," Phoenix added.

"With her best friend. And you thought you could get away with it?" Andy showed his pointed teeth, then let loose a roar that shook Mark like a sonic wave.

Phoenix leaned forward and hissed in Mark's ear. "Satan owns you now."

Mark began to cry. "I'm sorry!"

"You're not sorry enough," said Andy.

"I'll do anything!"

Andy and Phoenix exchanged looks.

Phoenix gave Andy a cheeky thumbs-up out of Mark's view.

Andy allowed himself a tiny smile. "You will pay her alimony on time. Every month."

Mark cowered silently.

"You will also give her enough extra money to remodel her kitchen."

Mark looked up. "Her kitchen?"

"DID I STUTTER?" roared Andy.

"No! Yes! Okay! Kitchen remodel, you got it!"

"You will never, ever cheat on a relationship partner again."

Mark nodded vigorously.

Andy glowered at the mortal at his feet. "If you do…"

"We will come for you!" Phoenix laughed maniacally.

Andy took hold of Mark's jaw. "And next time, it won't be so pleasant." He released his hold with a final push that knocked Mark sideways into an undignified sprawl.

Andy met Phoenix's gaze and gave a subtle nod.

The transformed demons faded from the dream and returned to their rooftop perch.

"I have to admit—that was pretty fun," said Phoenix. "Mind you, the costuming could have used some work."

"Picky," said Andy, smoothing his red suit self-consciously.

"You think he'll straighten up?"

Andy shrugged. "Who knows. At least Erin will get what she deserves."

"But will she get what she wants?"

Andy shot Phoenix a look. "What she wants is to move on and have a normal life."

"Normal's just an entry in the dictionary, mate."

Andy looked up at the night sky. "What do you believe, Phoenix?"

"Believe? I don't know. I believe you're giving me a headache."

"Demons don't get headaches," said Andy.

"I'm about to be the first."

"Do you remember before there were humans?" Andy paused. "I don't."

"So?"

"So what are we, really? Are we supernatural beings? Or are we what they imagine us to be?"

Phoenix turned an expression of skepticism on Andy. "They?"

"Humans. Mortals. Will we stop existing when they stop believing in us?"

Phoenix groaned. "You're bringing me down, Andy."

"I'm sorry. I'll stop."

"See that you do. And, anyway, if you think you're going to cease existing some time soon, perhaps you could knock off acting like a prat and try a little carpe diem, as the Romans used to say." Phoenix made a motion like plucking a piece of fruit from the air. "Besides, don't you have a wedding to go to?"

Andy got to his feet, balanced effortlessly on Mark's roof, and stretched his wings until the tips brushed the branches of the nearest tree. "You're absolutely right," he said.

PART III

ERIN & ANDROMALIUS

31

Erin woke to the scent of coffee and toast. She rolled over and sat up, letting her feet dangle over the edge of the bed. She checked to make sure Nancy Drew wasn't underfoot before easing her feet down to the floor.

The sound of Andy whistling in the kitchen carried through the closed bedroom door, along with the clinking sounds of cooking and table-setting.

She threw a robe over her pajamas and joined him in the kitchen.

"Good morning," said Andy. "Big day today." He carefully slid an omelet out of a hot pan onto a plate, then set the pan back on the burner.

"I feel a little weird about it." Erin slid into a chair at the kitchen table.

"That's because you need a good breakfast." Andy filled a mug with coffee and added cream and sugar. He placed the mug and the plate before her and turned back to the stove.

"Thanks." Erin lifted the mug and took a sip. It was exactly as she liked it. "I think I'm going to miss this."

"Miss what?" His back was to her as he whisked eggs in a bowl.

"This. Coffee. Company." She took a bite of the omelet. It was delicious, as usual. "I'll miss it."

He poured the beaten eggs into the pan. "I will, too."

"Where will you go?"

"Go?" He seemed to be slightly at a loss.

"What do demons do with their time off? Other than take massage lessons."

He stirred the eggs. "What would you do?"

"Me?" Erin considered. "I don't know. Travel? See the world? I've always wanted to go to Paris."

"That would be time well spent," said Andy. He folded the omelet and slid it onto a plate, then turned off the stove. He carried the plate to the table and sat across from Erin.

"But it would be more fun with a friend," she added.

He paused, fork in hand, and met her gaze. "Would it?"

She looked down and pushed the eggs around her plate. "I think it would."

Nancy Drew wandered into the kitchen.

Andy stood up and filled Nancy's food bowl, adding a small spoonful of plain cooked eggs to the dry food. "I forgot to tell you—I paid a little visit to your ex-husband last night." He sat down again.

Erin swallowed wrong and coughed. "Oh, my God. What did you do to him?"

"Nothing too harmful. I just put the fear of Andy into him. And the fear of Phoenix."

Erin laughed, which turned into more coughing. "I wish I'd been there."

"Let's just say your alimony payments will be very timely and the kitchen will get the remodeling of your dreams."

"Oh, Andy. I don't know how to thank you." She placed her hand over his and felt its radiant warmth. "You've done so much."

"Any demon would have done the same."

"I don't think that's true at all." Erin released his hand, stood up, and carried her empty plate to the sink. "Thank you for breakfast. And everything else." When she turned from the sink, she realized he'd been watching her intently.

"No—thank you," he said, with uncharacteristic gravity.

She retreated to the bedroom to shower, hoping the hot water would wash away the feelings that rippled through her like stones thrown in a pond. How was it possible to feel like you'd known someone forever, when your time together had passed in the blink of an eye?

Wrapped in a towel, Erin pushed aside the clothes in her closet to reach the new dress. She held it at arm's length, admiring the delicate blush color and subtle ombre shading, before laying it out carefully on the bed.

She applied her makeup and dried her hair. Then she slipped into the dress, fluffing its skirt and tugging the bodice into place. She reached for the zipper, but only managed to tug it halfway to the top despite contorting herself into a range of uncomfortable positions.

There was only one thing to do.

"Andy?" she called.

His voice came through the closed door slightly muffled. "Yes?"

"Can you help me?"

The door opened.

Andy entered, resplendent in a tan summer suit, holding a small white box in his hands.

"Can you…?" She gestured to the back of the dress.

He blinked and set the box down on the bed. "Of course!"

She felt his hands at her back, his fingers guiding the zipper upwards to close securely. She closed her eyes and tucked the memory of the sensation away, to remember after he was gone. "Thanks."

He opened his mouth as if to speak.

She thought he might thank her again.

Instead, he handed the box to her. "Here. I got this for you."

Erin opened the box. Inside, she found a corsage of fresh pink roses accented with a single salt-and-pepper-colored feather.

"Do you like it?" he said, shifting his weight from one foot to the other.

Erin lifted the corsage and inhaled the scent. "Of course I like it. Where did you get this?"

"I stopped by the rose garden at Destiny Park early this morning. They'll never miss a few roses here and there."

"A normal person might have stopped by the florist."

"I'm not normal. Or a person, technically." A bashful smile touched his lips.

She cradled the corsage in one hand and ran a finger over the feather. "No, you're not. But I think that's what I like about you."

At the ceremony, Andy could hardly sit still. Between shooting judgmental looks at Mark and Genevieve, and subtly checking on Erin out of the corner of his eye, he was a very distracted demon. Was she happy to be moving on? Unhappy to be reminded of past suffering? Andy considered removing Mark's pants one more time, just for good measure.

Honestly, the way Mark was sweating, it seemed like he was doing a fine job torturing himself. Genevieve looked a bit nauseous, too, although whether that could be chalked up to her pregnancy or proximity to someone like Mark was anyone's guess.

"All get what they want," Andy quoted under his breath. "They do not always like it."

Joyce, who was seated on the other side of Erin, leaned over. "Did you say something?" she whispered.

He shook his head and tried to convert his demonic smile into something more angelic.

When the pastor announced, "You may now kiss the bride," Andy snuck another look at Erin.

Her face appeared serene. Only around her eyes could he detect a hint of sadness. But what was she sad about? Mark's remarriage? Or could it be—something else?

She'd said she would miss him. She'd said she wanted a friend.

Could it be? Andy looked at her again, this time more directly.

She noticed. She smiled at him—and the sadness became clearer.

Andy barely noticed the bride and groom retreating down the aisle.

When the guests left the sanctuary for the reception hall, Andy followed Erin and Joyce. As the crowd mingled, he spotted a familiar face.

Make that two familiar faces.

Phoenix, dressed in an unusually conservative suit, and Raya, wearing an uncharacteristically demure dress, swanned through the reception hall as if they belonged there.

Andy slipped away from Erin and Joyce to intercept the wedding crashers. "What are you two doing here?"

"What does it look like we're doing?" said Phoenix. "Loading up on the free drinks."

"And free food," said Raya.

"You realize, of course, that this is a dry wedding?" said Andy.

Phoenix looked at him in disbelief. "A dry wedding? Who would do that to themselves?"

"At least there's lemonade."

Phoenix made a face.

Andy crossed his arms. "Do you want to tell me why you're really here, Phoenix?"

Phoenix leaned in and gripped Andy's shoulder. "Wouldn't leave you alone at a time like this, mate."

Raya patted the wand disguised as an accessory in her hair. "Plus, weddings are full of magic. Good place to stock up. Never know when it might come in handy."

"Try not to cause any trouble," said Andy.

"Oh, I can't make any promises." Phoenix grinned as Raya dragged him to the dance floor.

Andy found Erin at the refreshment table with her mother. He had to raise his voice over the rising noise of the crowd and the music. "Would you like to dance?"

"Sure!" said Erin. She reached for his hand.

He took it.

They skipped onto the dance floor and ran into Raya and Phoenix. Raya hugged Erin and lavished compliments on her new dress, before demonstrating a few of the latest dance moves, causing Erin to burst into a fit of giggles.

The foursome continued dancing to the reverberating pop music until the newlyweds finally made their appearance.

Genevieve stepped up onto the makeshift stage with her bouquet in her hands. She did a visible double take as she caught sight of Erin, smiling and laughing, one arm draped around Raya, the other around Andy, with Phoenix capering nearby like a madman, oblivious to anything else. Then she turned her back to the crowd as the DJ announced the throwing of the bouquet.

"Excuse me for a moment," Andy said to Erin. He made his way to the side of the stage and invisibly extended his wings. He watched Erin's gaze leave Genevieve and settle on him, taking in the view of his wings.

The look on her face was priceless.

Phoenix whispered something in Raya's ear, and they both stepped behind Erin, Phoenix giving Andy one more thumbs-up sign.

Genevieve flung the bouquet over her head without looking.

Andy flapped his wings once, hard, with a precision developed from centuries of flight.

The bouquet tumbled and changed direction in mid-air, buffeted by the wind from Andy's unseen wings, to land neatly at Erin's feet.

Erin, stunned, bent slowly to retrieve the bouquet. She wasn't looking at Genevieve at all. She looked only at the bouquet—and then she looked at him.

Even across the room, he found himself lost in the light of her eyes. Ignoring the stares of the crowd, he closed the distance between them and swept her into his arms. "Erin," he said, "you deserve everything. Every joy. Every happiness. And if I can share that with you—as your friend, as your *inamorato*—"

Erin made a sound like a laugh crossed with a sob.

"As whatever way you'd have me, I'd consider myself the luckiest of demons."

Tears streaked her cheeks, but she smiled—oh, how she smiled! "Andy, I don't know what eternity holds—but here and now, I want to hold *you*." Matching words to action, she held him even tighter, resting her head on his shoulder.

He could have held her until the sun flamed out, but the sound of Phoenix clearing his throat interrupted their blissful embrace.

"Disgusting, aren't they?" said Phoenix.

Raya punched him playfully in the shoulder. "I called it first."

"Thank you, Phoenix, for thoroughly ruining the moment," said Andy, drawing back from Erin, who laughed softly.

"Better me than her mother, who looks very interested in what you two are up to." Phoenix nodded in Joyce's direction as she made a beeline across the room.

"That's our cue to leave, I think. Shall we?" said Andy to Erin.

"Definitely."

They ran to the exit, laughing like schoolchildren, and escaped through the doors and into the bright light of the afternoon sun.

EPILOGUE

Erin placed the Christmas angel on the topmost tree branch and stepped back. It seemed a little strange to highlight an angel while celebrating Christmas with a demon—but then, nothing about her life had been particularly normal for quite some time.

Andy paused in the middle of fluffing the couch cushions to give the tree a once-over. "Wow," he said. "Accurate."

"Accurate?"

"The sword."

Erin's gaze returned to the angel. Sure enough, it held a long golden sword at its side. "I never even thought about it. Kind of odd for a holiday decoration to be wielding a sword."

Nancy Drew tottered to the front door and sat down with an air of expectation.

"I think someone's here," said Erin. She looked out the window and saw Raya's truck.

Raya approached, leading Blaze on a sturdy-looking leash.

Erin gently moved Nancy Drew out of the way and opened the door.

Blaze surged forward only to be stopped short by the leash.

"Blaze! Settle down," said Raya. She followed Erin to the back door and unclipped Blaze to run free in the backyard. Nancy Drew, already accustomed to Blaze from their occasional doggy playdates, wagged her tail happily and gave chase.

"Any word from Phoenix?" asked Erin.

Raya made a rude noise. "Probably skipping out on the whole thing, knowing him."

"Did someone say my name?" Phoenix materialized in an instant, right behind Raya.

She jumped and let out a small shriek before whirling to face him. "You—you demon! You know I hate it when you try to startle me."

"I know," he purred. "That's what makes it such fun." He sauntered out of the kitchen and found Andy adjusting the strings of Christmas tree lights. "You know this is extremely weird, right? Decorating for the enemy holiday? Putting an *angel* on your tree?" He looked closer. "And what kind of lunatic has an angel with a sword? How about a few elves with knives to round it out?"

Raya and Erin joined them.

"He's an idiot, but he does have a point," said Raya.

"Don't encourage him," said Andy. He stepped back and regarded his work.

Phoenix quickly stooped and shoved a package under the tree.

"What's that?" said Erin. "We said no gifts needed, remember?"

Phoenix looked away and mumbled something unintelligible.

"I'm sorry, I didn't quite catch that—"

"It's nothing." He threw himself on the couch and shot Andy a look. "Are you going to start the festivities, mate, or shall we stare at your dead tree some more?"

"Patience, my old demon friend. First, we have snacks—from Erin's newly remodeled kitchen!" Andy retreated to the kitchen and brought out two festive holiday trays.

Phoenix let out a dramatic sigh.

Erin and Raya snagged several exquisitely decorated Christmas cookies each. Erin took a seat on one end of the couch, and Raya sat cross-legged on the floor.

Andy seated himself on the couch between Phoenix and Erin. "Erin and I decided to open one present each for Christmas Eve, and we have a present for each of you, too."

Phoenix perked up. "I want my present."

Erin and Andy exchanged a grin. "I'll get it," said Erin. She went to the base of the tree and retrieved a rectangular box wrapped in bright red foil paper with a coordinating red ribbon.

Phoenix held out his hands like a greedy child. He took the box and shredded the paper, tossing it heedlessly in all directions. He pulled open the box and peered inside. "A bottle of wine?"

"It's the bottle you had when we summoned you. Remember?" said Erin.

He drew the bottle out of the box. "You took it away and wouldn't let me drink it."

"I found the identical vintage," said Andy.

Phoenix traced one finger over the label, a bemused look on his face.

"Why don't you open it?" said Raya.

"Like hell." Phoenix wrapped his arms protectively around the bottle. "This baby's all mine."

Raya rolled her eyes.

"And for you," Erin said, handing her a green-wrapped box.

"Ooh!" squealed Raya. She whipped off the ribbon and removed the lid. Tissue rustled; she flicked it out of the way and lifted a black t-shirt nestled within. "'Don't Make Me Drop a House on You'! I love it!"

Phoenix snatched the shirt and held it to his chest. "I think it would look better on me, actually."

Andy deftly snagged it and tossed it back to Raya. "Merry Christmas."

"Your turn," said Erin. She handed him a small, flat box wrapped in red.

Andy carefully peeled the tape away from one end.

"While we're young, Andromalius," said Phoenix.

"Hush," said Raya.

Andy removed the rest of the tape and unfolded the paper, laying it neatly to the side. The box lid came free to reveal a piece of heavy card stock with gold-embossed writing on it. "Make & Take: Using Power Tools to Make a Cutting Board. A class!"

"You like it?"

Andy kissed her cheek soundly. "I love it." He reached for another package. "Now yours."

Instead of wrapping paper, the present was wrapped and tied in candy cane-striped fabric. Erin released the bow and folded back the fabric.

A cloth-bound photo album lay inside.

Erin glanced at Andy, who gave her an encouraging smile. She ran her fingers over the cover before opening it.

The photos began with back-to-school week, when Andy returned to help her finish her new classroom before the first day of school. There they were—posing by the blackboard, dusty and rumpled and grinning for the camera. Then Halloween, with Raya and Erin dressed as witches, and Phoenix and Andy wearing fake devil horns. Thanksgiving—when Erin's mother crashed their Thanksgiving party and flirted shamelessly with Phoenix, much to his chagrin.

The last page held a single photo from immediately after Mark and Genevieve's terrible, wonderful wedding.

Erin and Andy were still in their finery, sitting on a boulder in a nearby park, the wedding bouquet in her hands. They faced each other under the bright afternoon sun, grinning like fools.

Erin's eyes pricked, and the photo blurred. She turned to Andy.

He held a bright sprig of mistletoe. He lifted it in the air with one hand and brought his other arm gently around her, holding her close. "Every day with you is a gift I cherish. I love you, Erin."

She pressed her lips to his, and the tear that had gathered at the corner of her eye overflowed. A touch of salt baptized their kiss. Andy's cinnamon scent and unearthly warmth wrapped her so sweetly it made the demonic seem like heaven.

"Oh, for the love of all that's unholy—knock it off, you two," said Phoenix.

Raya threw a pillow at him.

Erin and Andy came up for air with a shared laugh.

"One more present," said Andy. He rose and went to the back door. "Nancy Drew! Blaze!"

Nancy Drew was closest to the door, and toddled amiably inside.

Blaze blasted through the door like a canine freight train. She ran a circuit of the living room and bumped into the Christmas tree, setting the angel wobbling on its perch. Then she leaped into Phoenix's lap.

"Raya! Get this slobbering hellbeast off me!"

"Down, Blaze," said Raya.

Blaze settled at her feet and laid her large head on Raya's knee.

Erin scooped up Nancy Drew and patted her.

Andy emerged from the kitchen with two cellophane holiday bags tied with string and stuffed with what looked like cookies. He shook the bags proudly. "For our good girls!"

Phoenix snorted.

Raya and Erin shared a look.

"Not you," clarified Andy. "Our furry babies." He opened a treat bag, pulled out a dog treat, and fed it to Nancy Drew. "I made them myself." He handed the other bag to Raya.

"That's so thoughtful, Andy—thank you!" She gave Blaze a treat.

Blaze crunched it up in seconds.

"Oh—what about Phoenix's present?" said Erin.

"It's nothing," he said. He got up, pulled it out from under the now-crooked tree, and handed it nonchalantly to Raya.

Raya took it with wide eyes. "For me?"

"Like I said, it's nothing."

"I thought you weren't into enemy holidays," said Andy.

"Shut up, demon," said Phoenix.

Raya, momentarily stunned by the unexpected gift, set into motion slowly. She removed the paper and revealed a garment box. She pulled off the lid. "The black dress from the mall! How did you know my size?"

"Oh, well, you know . . ." Phoenix seemed to be looking everywhere but at Raya. "Can't have you wandering around in t-shirts all the time, can we?"

For once, Raya seemed at a loss for words.

"Picture time!" said Andy. He jumped up and propped up a camera across from the couch.

Erin scooted down with Nancy Drew. Andy returned to the couch. Raya hopped up, followed by Blaze, and took the space between Andy and Phoenix, with Blaze on the floor in front of her.

"Do I have to?" said Phoenix.

"Shut up and smile," said Raya.

"Say 'Merry Christmas'!" added Erin as the camera counted down with a series of beeps.

When the countdown was almost up, Andy, Erin, and Raya chorused "Merry Christmas!"

"Happy Halloween," said Phoenix, rebelliously.

The camera flashed.

They released their pose and broke into laughter.

When the laughter subsided, and Phoenix and Raya had become occupied in a spirited debate on the relative merits of witch magic versus demon magic, Erin turned to Andy. She traced the line of his salt-and-pepper beard. "I love you, Andy. Merry Christmas."

He kissed her. It lasted even longer than the previous kiss.

And this time, even Phoenix didn't try to interrupt.

Continue the fun with *A Witch's Work Is Never Done*!

About the Author

Kate Moseman is a writer, photographer, and recipe developer who lives in Florida with her family.

www.ingramcontent.com/pod-product-compliance
Lightning Source LLC
LaVergne TN
LVHW041802080425
808058LV00004B/520